To Peggy—
Blessings on your
journey with the
Remember He is my
away.   Ellen Scott 2/18/03

FOR THE LOVE OF PADAH

For the LOVE of PADAH

EILEEN SCOTT

PADAH PRESS

FOR THE LOVE OF PADAH

Published by

Padah Press

© 2003 by Eileen Scott

All of Eileen Scott's books can be ordered

through her website at www.eileenscott.com

email: info@eileenscott.com

Telephone Orders: 1-866-774-5395

Have your VISA or MasterCard ready

Postal Orders: Padah Press

P.O. Box 1289, Gresham, OR 97030

ISBN 0-9721269-0-2

Library of Congress Control Number 2002101806

Book Cover, Book Design and Illustration

by Robilyn Robbins

Cover: detail from: "Sierra Nevada Morning"

by Albert Bierstadt c. 1870. Oil on canvas, 46" x 84". 0126.2305

from the collection of the

Thomas Gilcrease Institute of American History and Art

Tulsa, Oklahoma. Used by permission.

Editor: Victoria McCown

Printed in the United States of America

TO MY CHILDREN,
JEREMY, NATHAN, AND AMANDA:

You have brought

so much joy into my life.

With love,

I dedicate this book to you.

CONTENTS

ACKNOWLEDGEMENTS

In admiring the finished work of a tapestry, one can barely discern the countless individual threads woven together. Yet each thread plays an important part in creating the whole, weaving its unique and invaluable contribution throughout the piece, not for individual glory, but for the sake of the whole.

This book, too, is like a tapestry, finely woven with the kind wishes and hard work of those who have invested so much of themselves on my behalf for its production. You are my parents and family, my friends, and my business associates, without whom this story would never have been told. Thank you for your prayers, encouragement, and faith in me.

I want to acknowledge my Aunt Pat for her assistance and prayerful support; my friends Jan and Michelle, who encouraged me through each and every chapter; my daughter Amanda, who faithfully read every word, proving herself my most loyal fan; my son Nathan for his lattés; Jeremy, for his encouragement; and Bently, my sheltie, who although he has no idea of his honorable mention, spent many hours at my feet as I wrote late into the night.

Thank you, Dr. Lynda Falkenstein, for your mentoring, wisdom, and inspiration; and Robilyn, for your artistic design and willing heart.

Above all, I would like to thank my gracious Heavenly Father for His priceless investment in my life. Thank you for giving me the opportunity to share our story.

INTRODUCTION

Over fifteen years ago, the first chapter of Padah's story was written for a group of children and adults at the request of a staff member from the church our family attended. Little did I realize at the time of the request the personal relevance of the assignment nor the role it would play in my future. Once completed, the story was set aside for over a decade, yet the character of Padah continued to live on in my heart. Her untold story refused to be quieted.

As with many of us, life's journey, traveled one day at a time, teaches its most profound lessons from the perspective of hindsight. It is the view, once we finally reach the summit, that makes our heart glad and we rejoice in our shepherd's incredible wisdom and faithfulness.

Thus, the story of Padah was written in the depths of my heart, soul, and spirit, between the mountains and valleys of life. Although an allegory told through the eyes of a sheep, it is in truth a very personal story, spanning a number of years spent in the loving care of the Great Shepherd. Through the tears and pain of personal loss and trauma, as well as the moments of peace, joy, and victory, the Great Shepherd has led, from tragedy to triumph. And it is because of His countless mercies and incomparable love alone that this sheep has lived to declare His praises.

May this story be an encouragement to all who have traveled such a path.

Eileen Scott

PADAH

If there were a fate worse than ending up in the old man's pasture, Padah certainly could not imagine what it might be. Cautiously she approached the rusty woven-wire fence which held her friend Mara captive on the other side. Disturbed by her friend's condition, Padah watched helplessly as the pathetic, underfed sheep struggled to stand on her feet. Mara, obviously distraught, continued to stare blankly through the wires at the lush pastures that lay beyond her reach.

"He will come for you too," Padah whispered, "I promise he will!" But Mara, whose name meant "bitter waters," appeared unconsoled by Padah's gentle words of encouragement. "The kind shepherd never forgets his promises. You just can't give up!"

Slowly the bedraggled sheep's eyes met with Padah's. "Oh...to be set free at last from that awful man!" Mara moaned, briefly entertaining the thought, only to dismiss it just as quickly. "You forget, Padah! I am a skinny old ewe well past my lamb-bearing years, and I am of little use to anyone any more."

"That's where you're wrong," Padah insisted. "The kind shepherd is not at all like the old man!"

Mara looked nothing like she once did, before the old man claimed her. Her dark sunken eyes and twisted frame were painful reminders of her years of abuse. Padah could only imagine what her own destiny might have been had she not been rescued on that dreadful day not all that long ago. The memories still haunted her, the sheer horror remained much too vivid in her mind.

The hot afternoon had been cloudy, much like this one. A threatening summer storm unexpectedly triggered the old man's fury, which he had unleashed on the unsuspecting, weary flock. Known throughout the valley for both his cruelty and the neglectfulness of his sheep, the old man had beaten them mercilessly with his rod as he drove them down the dusty road toward home.

"Yaw! Yaw! Move, you lazy beasts!" he had screamed impatiently. "I'll not be caught in the rain again this time because of you!"

The loud crack of his rod had pierced the wind as if to compete with the lightning strikes that zigzagged across the dark sky. The thunderous roar of hooves that surrounded Padah nearly drowned out the deafening clap of thunder from the approaching storm. Her thin legs shook violently beneath her small frame and her heart raced with fear as if it were about to leap from her chest. If only she could keep up with the rest of the herd, she told herself, she would not be overtaken by their madness.

As thick black dust swirled up into her face, clouding her vision, the smell of fresh sweat filled her nostrils. She could hardly catch her breath and a sickening wave of fear took hold of her stomach. Nearly overwhelmed with panic, Padah had forced herself to look straight ahead, when her left front hoof twisted, penetrating a deep hole beneath her. Despite efforts to pull herself free, the hard, unforgiving earth refused to relinquish its grasp. The sharp stabbing pain in her injured ankle rippled through the length of her body. Padah collapsed to the ground. Trampled by the rest of the terrified sheep, she was soon left behind, utterly alone and suffering unbelievable agony.

Suddenly the old man turned around and walked swiftly back toward her. Thankful that she had been noticed, Padah's fears lessened and hope filled her heart. Nothing could have prepared her for what came next.

With a disgusted grunt the old man carelessly yanked her right leg from the hole only to heartlessly heave her to the side of the road.

"You are worth nothing to me alive!" he hollered. "But the butcher will pay me well. And your skin and wool will keep me warm against the winter winds!"

Turning abruptly to leave, he grumbled in disgust, "I'll be back soon for the carcass."

Horrified, Padah began to quiver with fright, her uncontrollable sobs unable to communicate the depths of her broken heart.

The black, threatening clouds overhead wasted no time spilling their rain upon the dry rocky land. And the thundershowers, which filled the ditches to overflowing, raced swiftly over the mountain range, leaving behind only the small, dejected sheep that lay limp in the mud-soaked grass.

As the skies cleared, the kind shepherd, having business on his mind that day, set out on his journey into town. He had not traveled far, however, when the sheep's anguished cries caught his attention. Walking to the side of the road, his eyes quickly scanned the deep grass. Spying the small sheep, the kind shepherd knelt down beside her. He could not help but notice her extreme thinness, nor her badly broken leg as he ran a comforting hand over her side. Beneath her dirty wool coat, he could feel numerous open sores.

"It must be the old man again! No doubt he is the one responsible for such ruthless neglect!" he whispered under his breath.

Recognizing the helpless condition of the little lamb, the tenderhearted shepherd gently reached down to pick her up. Within seconds, her desperate bleating began to subside. Cradling her in his arms, he affectionately stroked her dirty, matted wool as a promise formed on his lips.

"This is one sheep that despicable man who calls himself a shepherd will not have!"

With firm resolve he set out in the direction of the old man's house at the end of the valley. But before he could knock, the door flew open. Supporting Padah's broken body in his arms, the shepherd spoke first.

"I have come to purchase this one small sheep."

"So! You have come to take another one for yourself? Do you not have already enough sheep of your own? Enough to graze on all your many acres?" the old man hissed jealously. "Your flocks cover the highlands. They graze on the best land as far as any eye can see and your streams never dry up, even during times of drought! Yet you still

4

are not satisfied and you meddle where you do not belong! Take another sheep from me and I shall never forget, nor will the rest of the valley by the time I have finished informing them of your insatiable greed!"

Undisturbed by the old man's threats, the kind shepherd silently reached into his robe and pulled out a large leather pouch. All the money he possessed was within that pouch. Without hesitation he offered it to the old man who angrily snatched the bag.

"You will pay for this more than once!"

The generous shepherd did not seem to care. The small sheep now belonged to him. Taking part of his robe, the shepherd immediately tied the lamb closely to his side. From that day on he called her "Padah," which meant "to ransom, to deliver, to rescue surely."

"*Do not be afraid,*
for I have ransomed you.
I have called you by name; you are mine."
—Isaiah 43:1 NLT

C H A P T E R   T W O

EW BEGINNINGS

TWO YEARS AFTER PADAH'S RESCUE

Spring arrived early on the highlands of Menuca, eagerly dismissing the customary cold winter rains. Despite lack of normal precipitation, the richness and beauty of the land remained undeniable. Menuca, a place of unusual stillness and peace, literally meant "resting place." Here the kind shepherd tended his flocks.

It was one of those wonderful warm nights in spring, when the sky like black velvet revealed every star in the heavens. And the moon, as it cast its light upon a nearby stream, gave the illusion of a thousand shimmering diamonds. A gentle breeze rustled the tender leaves of the trees and spread the sweet smell of new grass everywhere.

Several hours had passed since sundown and the sheep of the kind shepherd now rested safely within the walls of the sheepfold. Some of these were newborn lambs cuddling close to their mother's side. So quiet was the night that only the occasional tinkling of sheep bells broke the blissful silence.

Off in the corner, Padah, who was about to become a mother for the first time, struggled bravely in her effort to give birth. Exhausted after many hours of hard labor, she rested her weary head in the hand of the kind shepherd. Kneeling beside her, he reassuringly stroked her side.

"I know it is hard, my little one, but do not become discouraged and give up. Very soon you shall have a wee one of your own to nestle at your side," he gently encouraged.

Despite having spent many long hours of hard work on the grassy slopes that day, the shepherd refused to leave Padah's side for even a moment. No one else could give her what he could. And although he showed no partiality among his sheep, he could not deny that this little one occupied a cherished place in his heart. Her desire to obey him and her need for closeness had set her apart from the others. Wherever the shepherd went he could always count on her being no further than two feet from his heels, the bell around her neck tinkling gaily as she pranced along.

Looking down upon her small frame, now heavy with lamb, he found it difficult to believe that she was the same mangled, pathetic sheep he had found along the roadside only two years earlier. Despite her recovery, the time spent in the old man's pasture had weakened her condition. Padah, it appeared, would always walk with a limp. However, her obvious imperfection seemed of little concern to the kind shepherd, for it was her heart that he truly valued.

Now the moment of birth had arrived. Joyous anticipation flooded the shepherd's heart at the thought of beholding Padah's first offspring. Would she bear another just like herself? he wondered.

Suddenly a small shrill bleat brought his attention back to the present. Lying in the straw before him was a perfectly formed white lamb. It was strong, healthy, and, knowing instinctively what to do first began nursing with tremendous gusto. The shepherd named him "Zachar" which meant "to still think on; to remember."

"So, you could not wait any longer to see the world for yourself, Zak?" the kind shepherd chuckled as he gently patted the lively newborn on his small head.

Moments later a second lamb also emerged from Padah's womb. Although mostly white, on his left side he wore a large black patch of wool that did not seem to belong there at all. And unlike his twin brother, his small frail body lay motionless at the feet of his mother. There was no greeting cry nor wet wiggling form to signal life. The slight, delicate figure did not struggle to its feet to gain use of his new legs. His eyes remained closed. He did not breathe. Desperate and afraid, Padah's eyes quickly sought out those of the kind shepherd.

"It's okay, Padah," the shepherd reassured. "He's a wee little one and very weak from the long birth, but we'll give him a bit of help. You'll see!"

Swiftly the shepherd reached out for the tiny lamb and turned it on its side. Clearing the small animal's throat with his finger, the kind shepherd gently grasped the lamb by the nose so that his thumb and fingers were slightly above the surface of the nostrils. As he inflated the lungs of the baby lamb by blowing gently, the shepherd breathed his own breath into the tiny lifeless form. Carefully, he pushed down on the lamb's chest to expel the air.

With patience and determination, the shepherd continued the process in an effort to revive the tiny figure. Finally, a faint cry escaped the baby lamb's lips. The shepherd returned the lamb to Padah's side to nurse, but weak as it was, the tiny newborn could not suckle. Helplessly, Padah looked up into the eyes of the shepherd once again.

This time the shepherd softly laughed. "So, you have given me a second gift, but you want me feed him for you! Well, he's going to have to work hard to keep up with his big brother!"

The shepherd placed a small amount of Padah's own milk on his thumb, drizzling a few drops onto the newborn's tongue. Inserting his thumb into the lamb's mouth, the shepherd wet-nursed the little one. He decided to name the small lamb "Nakeh," for it meant "dejected, contrite, and humble."

With a knowing smile that radiated both love and tenderness, he whispered into the young lamb's ear. "I can see already, my little one, that you are going to be just like your mother."

"*For the Spirit of God has made me;*
and the breath
of the Almighty gives me life."
—*Job 33:4 NIV*

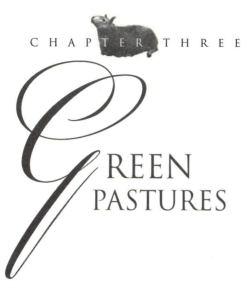

CHAPTER THREE

G REEN PASTURES

Happy and content, Padah's heart swelled with pride at having her own babes. Warmth radiated from the two soft figures now tucked tightly by her side, and thankfulness overwhelmed her heart. Maybe, she thought, just maybe, this would finally fill the emptiness within her. Nothing could be more satisfying than motherhood, and certainly nothing more important! She had found her place of belonging.

The night had been long and the hours of sleep short, but Padah lifted her eyes in search of the kind shepherd's whereabouts. As usual he rested at the entrance of the sheepfold, his presence a constant reminder of selfless devotion to his beloved flock.

There were so many things Padah did not yet know about her kind shepherd, but of one truth she was certain. Her destiny was entirely dependent upon the mercy and continuous care of her owner. The touch of the kind shepherd's hand upon her head reached into the very depths of her soul, both healing her heart and calming her fears. She could not imagine any place safer than being held in his arms or wrapped in his cloak.

Another day was about to begin, and despite only faint morning light, the lush green pastures beyond the sheepfold already glistened, heavy-laden with dew. Their abundant grasses swayed freely back and forth in the breeze, as if to tempt the flocks to partake of their rich pleasures. Padah had only dreamed of nibbling such succulent grasses while in the barren confines of the neglectful old man's property. Unlike the sparse, dry, tasteless stocks of the past, the rich green blankets of grass in the kind shepherd's pastures tasted delightfully sweet and tender. They satisfied like nothing she had ever known before.

With the sudden departure of winter and the fullness of spring descending upon Menuca, the surrounding hillsides were draped in a vast array of daffodils, wild baby iris, lush green beds of moss, and purple heather. Butterflies danced about, resting with sheer delight upon the fresh new leaves of spring. Without question, spring was Padah's favorite time of year. Now she had her own two lambs with whom to celebrate the newness of life!

On this particular morning, several other flocks of sheep, all belonging to different owners, shared the same walled quarters of the sheepfold with the kind shepherd and his flock. The four-foot-high walls of the sheepfold both discouraged thieves and provided protection from predators. Constructed with stones gathered from the fields and topped with thorns, this particular sheepfold was located on the northernmost corner of the kind shepherd's land.

Unfortunately, the sparse winter showers had produced very little rainfall. The short supply of water already presented a problem for many of the shepherds in the Valley of Achor, which literally meant "Trouble Valley." Countless times the kind shepherd had offered to share his streams and pastures in the highlands of Menuca with the others in need.

Awake now, the kind shepherd slowly rose to his feet, as did the others. All the sheep in the fold began to stir, their eyes and ears fixed expectantly at the entrance of the sheepfold. As each shepherd stepped outside the compound, a loud piercing cry would emanate from his lips. Immediately, the sheep twisted and turned within the group. Out filed that particular shepherd's flock obediently gathering at his feet.

To an outside observer, each herder's shrill call sounded identical. To the sheep, however, it was unique. Not only did they recognize their master's voice, but they refused to even acknowledge another. It was as if they did not hear any other call. A stranger they would not follow.

With the twins fed, Padah encouraged them to stand.

"Zak, you try it first! The time has come to follow the shepherd into the meadows that are fresh with dew. We must leave before the sun gets too high in the sky and the heat too intense."

A bit wobbly at first, Zak managed to stand on all four legs without much effort. Excitedly, his tail swung rapidly back and forth. But for Nakeh it was not quite so easy, his hesitancy obvious to his big brother.

"Come on, Nakeh, what are you waiting for?" Zak coached. "You can do it. Look at me!" Zak gave Nakeh a second demonstration of his newfound coordination.

Attempting to emulate his brother, Nakeh forced himself to stand up, only to fall backward onto his small rear.

"It's okay, Nakeh. Not everyone is successful at first. Just try it again," Padah encouraged.

But Nakeh's awkward legs simply refused to cooperate. It was if they were made of soft rubber and folded underneath him with every effort he made to stand. Finally, he landed on the ground with a frightful thud. Frustrated and disappointed, he began to cry.

Seeing this, the kind shepherd addressed him. "Nakeh, won't you ride on top my shoulders as I lead the group today?"

Me, sit on the shoulders of the kind shepherd? Nakeh thought to himself.

"I need you to ride on top of my shoulders so that the others can see you and know where to follow," the shepherd explained. "You will do that for me, won't you?"

Small Nakeh did not know what to say, except yes. After all, he could not refuse the shepherd. Besides, sitting atop his shoulders might just have its benefits on such a long journey.

With ease, the shepherd lifted Nakeh and placed the small lamb on his shoulders. Holding the sheep's front legs on one side and hind legs on the other, the shepherd wore him like a collar. The shepherd's firm grip on Nakeh's legs made him feel safe and secure. With Padah and Zak following close behind, the kind shepherd walked to the entrance of the sheepfold.

As the shepherd stood in the threshold of the doorway, Nakeh proudly observed the rest of the flock from his new strategic position upon the shepherd's shoulders. Summoning the rest of his flock, the kind shepherd slowly led them out into the vast pasture.

The morning sun was already sharing some of its warmth. Though early spring, the day would soon be hot. Knowing this, the shepherd chose the path along the creek bed which bordered the old man's property. The sheep would need the water once the dew had evaporated from the grass and leaves.

Padah soon spotted Mara pressing her nose against the same rusty fence they had shared previously. As if reading Padah's unspoken thoughts, her friend Joy joined her side.

"There is nothing you can do, Padah. It is more than a woven-wire fence that stands in the way of Mara's freedom."

"But it's so sad. I know how she feels. I met her when I lived in the valley. Has she ever been outside the old man's pasture at all?"

"Once, many years ago," replied Joy. "She was born in the old man's pasture, but gained her freedom at one point, coming to live with the kind shepherd."

"What happened?" Padah inquired.

"Well, one day she got in the way of not only Ursula, but Zula, and there was a terrible fight. They both took her on! You know how arrogant and domineering those old ewes can be," Joy shook her head. "Despite their length of time with the kind shepherd, they still insist on clinging to their old ways."

"Go on," urged Padah.

"Mara tried to stand her ground rather than be bullied, but Zula rammed her unmercifully. She forced her backward right off the edge of the cliff. Mara fell to the foot of the canyon ending up right back on the old man's property. It was months before anyone saw or heard from her again."

"How terrible!" Padah shuddered.

"Yes. Now she says she'd rather live in the old man's pasture until the day she dies than to have to share quarters with the kind shepherd's sheep again."

"If you can call that living!" Padah interjected.

"Unfortunately, it appears she'd rather drink from those filthy bitter waters than be free."

"Even if it means death from the parasites that could drive her mad?" Padah asked.

"Padah, sometimes freedom is a choice, and even though it is difficult to understand how someone could refuse such a gift, Mara has."

"What about the shepherd? Did he go in search of her?"

"The kind shepherd searched for her for two days, without rest. When he finally found her, she wouldn't accept his help and refused to return with him."

Unwilling to give up, Padah whispered, "Certainly there must be something we can do. We can't just leave her there! I can't stand the thought!"

"Padah, believe it or not, there is something worse than ending up in the old man's pasture and living in the Valley of Achor. But that is something only you can discover for yourself."

Perplexed, Padah decided it was best to drop the subject for now.

Joy, who was not only very wise, had become someone with whom Padah shared a deep bond of affection. It was Joy who stood by her so many times when the ewes made fun of her limp. And it was Joy who shared her sorrows and triumphs and taught her many lessons about her own journeys with the shepherd. If there were one sheep in the flock Padah could trust, it was Joy.

"Look at your son now," Joy giggled. "He has certainly caught on quickly!" Confidently racing ahead, leaping over anything in his path, Zak was in pure ecstasy exploring his wondrous new world.

"Weeee...Hey, Nakeh, look at this. I can jump almost as high as the fence!" Zak boasted as he flung his hind legs up in the air. Spotting a bright orange butterfly, he darted from flower to flower trying to catch the insect with his tongue. As if to tease the young lamb, the butterfly moved rapidly to a fresh clump of wildflowers. Not willing to give up the chase or be outdone, Zak took a flying leap across the mud puddle that separated him from the butterfly.

Fearing the obvious, Padah could hardly bring herself to watch. However, Nakeh, who was still on the shepherd's shoulders, looked on in amazement, harboring a bit of admiration for the courage and zest his brother possessed.

"That's the way. Get him, Zak!" Nakeh cheered exuberantly.

Suddenly Zak's gleeful ride through the air stopped embarrassingly short—but not short enough to avoid colliding with Zula, showering her in a spray of mud.

"Oops!" Nakeh himself couldn't help but cringe.

"Oh, no! He would have to run into Zula!" Padah murmured. "I will probably never hear the end of this."

"You know better than to let Zula get the best of you," Joy reminded her.

As anticipated, and unwilling to miss her opportunity, Zula started in.

"How utterly disgraceful!" she bellowed. "Certain sheep simply don't have the skills for parenting! I guess that's to be expected from those with less than acceptable breeding!"

Casting an angry glance at Padah, Zula continued to grumble as she walked away, leaving the other sheep to graze. Zak, avoiding further exploits, refused to stray from his mother's side the remainder of the afternoon. Evening came quickly, and even Nakeh had to admit there had been more than enough excitement for one day.

"My people will live in peaceful dwelling places, in secure homes, in undisturbed places of rest."
—Isaiah 32:18 NLT

ℰARMARKED

The previous day's travel proved long and hot, but none complained. Moving the sheep between meadows was necessary to avoid over-grazing problems. And by now, though it had been nearly two days' journey from the northernmost corner of Menuca back to the shepherd's cottage, an unmistakable sense of tranquility was felt by all. This was the place the sheep and their shepherd called home.

No one knew exactly how long the kind shepherd's farm had graced the highlands of Menuca, because none could remember a time when he wasn't there. The sturdy, well-manicured appearance of the cottage had always been a welcome relief for weary travelers passing by. Those who visited remarked that the generosity of the shepherd's heart was exceeded only by the deep bond of affection he held for his sheep.

The stone exterior of the modest cottage stood solidly, softened by both its straw roof and an abundance of ivy. The lead paned windows often glowed late into the night from the lamps that burned within, accompanied by smoke from the tall brick chimney curling into the evening air. The barn stood conveniently close by.

Purposely returning his flocks to the farm, the kind shepherd turned to the task of marking them as his own. Though far from pleasant, this necessary ritual protected the sheep and master. Each shepherd had his own distinctive earmark, which he cut into one of the ears of his sheep. In this way, even at a distance, one could easily determine to whom the sheep belonged.

Each ewe must first be secured prior to placing its ear on a wooden block. The ear was notched deeply with the razor-sharp edge of the knife. Despite a painful process for both sheep and shepherd, the result of mutual suffering produced an indelible mark of ownership that could never be erased. Every sheep that came into the possession of the kind shepherd bore his unique mark.

As she waited, Padah stood anxiously by the fence, her eyes focused on the shepherd, who held the knife in his hand. With her stomach knotted tight in apprehension, Padah fought intensely her natural inclination to flee.

Whatever can the shepherd be thinking of? Padah thought to herself.

"So you're actually going to become one of us?" Zula sneered. "How positively delightful."

Ursula, an older ewe and a friend of Zula, took her turn. "I just hope you and your unruly brood can keep up with the rest of the flock!"

Sensing Padah was upset, Zula continued to taunt her. "Don't make the mistake of thinking that just because he rescued you that you are any different than the rest of us. Your limp will not gain you any extra sympathy around here. In fact, you may find yourself serving the master in an entirely different way than you anticipated, if you know what I mean."

"That's not true," Padah countered.

"Isn't it? You don't think he'd keep you here out of the mere goodness of his heart! After all, we are just sheep, and you're just one of how many?"

"Stop it!" Padah cried out.

"Oh, that would be such a loss! Yes, it would be a terrible loss," she said, shaking her head as she lowered it. "And to think what might happen to your twins!"

Overhearing Zula's cruel attempt to stir up self-doubt and fear, Joy walked over to Padah and gave her a comforting nuzzle.

"Ignore her," Joy said quietly. "That's the only way she knows how to maintain her position among the flock. She demeans the other sheep, but she is the one riddled with inferiority and fear. Her arrogance is her way of trying to dominate the rest of us."

"But the others follow her example and look up to her," Padah continued.

"It is tragic because her name actually means 'leader.' She hasn't a clue that to truly be a leader you must first serve others. Her pride will do her in faster than the knife ever will. Pride is a horrible defect in sheep, Padah, something that even the kind shepherd will not tolerate for long. The others may look and judge from the outside, but the shepherd looks far deeper. He understands our secret struggles, and he is the only one worth caring about."

"Why does he allow her to continue?" Padah questioned.

"His love is greater than ours. He understands her pain and has plans for her. His hope is that she will learn his ways."

"And if she doesn't?" Padah countered.

"She will no longer be able to remain with his flock."

Padah's eyes betrayed an inner turmoil. She looked anxiously at the shepherd.

"Joy, what is the kind shepherd doing with that dreadful knife? He wouldn't really use it on us, would he?" she asked.

"He will have to, Padah, but not in the way Zula suggested. You must allow him to place his mark on your ear. It will hurt at first and blood will follow, but it is the only way you can become part of the shepherd's family. After he has placed his mark on you, ownership will never be a question again. The kind shepherd would always find you if you ever lost your way. Without the shepherd's earmark, the old man could find you and claim you as his own permanently. Not only could you lose your freedom, but possibly never see your twins again."

At that moment the shepherd's shadow passed over Padah, making her aware of his presence. As she lifted her head and looked up into his deep blue eyes, something quite unexpected drew her in. An overwhelming sense of love, very different from anything she had ever experienced, captured her heart. Although afraid of the marking procedure, she suddenly realized that what appeared to be a horrifying event was in truth an act of love. Lifting her up with his strong arms, the kind shepherd carried Padah over to the large blood-stained block of wood. She would not resist but endure the pain if it meant forever belonging to him, because to be without the kind shepherd had become unthinkable.

The twins soon followed, each one receiving the kind shepherd's mark of ownership. Because many new lambs had been born into the shepherd's flock that spring, earmarking took the entire day. With nightfall close, returning to the comfortable old barn became a pleasurable thought. Padah felt most anxious to settle down to nurse her lambs.

Joy, walking not far behind, made her way to the barn as well. Together they settled into the fresh straw. Ursula soon joined them.

"Joy?"

"Yes, Padah?"

"Have you always belonged to the kind shepherd?"

"No. I, too, lived captive among the flocks of the old man a very long time ago. I can remember as if it were yesterday...a most frightful experience!"

Padah considered Joy's answer. Unlike the others, Joy was not timid and fearful, as were most sheep. Her peaceful appearance did not reflect the years of abuse.

"I know what you're thinking, Padah. I should somehow be sad or frightened because of my experience. But when the shepherd gave me a new beginning, he took my sadness and turned my mourning into joy! Like you, he gave me a new name."

She smiled at Padah, her kind eyes warm.

"It is late, Padah. We will talk again in the morning. I have something very special to share with you, but first we must get plenty of rest."

"Come, let us bow down in worship,
let us kneel before the Lord our Maker; for he is
our God and we are the people of his pasture,
the flock under his care."
–Psalm 95:6-7 NIV

THE  EETING PLACE

The sound of men's voices outside the barn awakened Padah before dawn. Although one of them sounded familiar, she could not distinguish to whom it belonged because of the distance. Not yet ready to break the stillness, Padah listened intently, while the other sheep lay sleeping, unaware of the presence of strangers.

As the men drew nearer, however, the morning breeze picked up their voices and carried the words in Padah's direction.

"Of course he moved the property line in his favor!" one man said.

"If we don't stick together we stand to lose everything in this drought," added another. "It's only spring and already we are wanting. Without the usual mountain runoff, there will never be enough water. It could be the end of us all!"

"Why do you think he's been so generous? Surely no one will question what he's been up to that way! He wants all the water for himself. And, how many of you have sheep you've lost but can't explain why?"

Stunned, Padah recognized the voice. It belonged to the old man!

"He's the only one with enough water to last through the summer and fall," the old man continued. "Mark my words, it is not from his land that he draws the water! It is my stream that he redirected at the headwaters. And I won't be the only one suffering if he's not stopped!"

Padah could hardly believe her ears.

"Joy! Wake up! Joy, you've got to listen!" Padah pleaded.

Joy began to stir, but the voices trailed off as the men walked away. Morning light would soon expose the strangers' presence.

"What's the reason for such panic at this hour?" Joy asked Padah, yawning.

"I woke up because I heard men's voices outside. One of them was the old man. Something is very wrong," Padah told her.

"Why? What was he saying?"

"He was telling the others that the kind shepherd was cheating and stealing from them by moving the property line!"

"Certainly there must be a mistake, Padah. That does not sound like the shepherd at all. If there is a problem, the kind shepherd will find out about it soon enough and settle the matter. Besides, it's not something that you or I can do anything about. Our place is to trust."

"Maybe I was overreacting a bit because of my fear," Padah admitted. "Ever since I escaped from that old man's place I've been afraid he will return for me someday."

"I've felt the same thing about him myself," Joy agreed. "Despite that feeling, you must remind yourself that you are safe here. As long as you stay close to the kind shepherd, there is nothing the old man can do to harm you." She paused then said, "Remember that I told you I had something special to share with you? When you have finished feeding your twins it will be time for us to go out into the fields. I will show you then."

Unable to imagine what Joy could possibly want to show her, Padah's curiosity grew.

As the kind shepherd entered the barn, his warmth and enthusiasm lifted any apprehension remaining in Padah's mind. His soft smile and easy laugh completely set her fears to rest.

How could anyone even question his goodness? she thought to herself. No one could if they really knew him.

The kind shepherd, now ready to lead his flock out to graze, opened the doors wide, allowing the first rays of sunlight to filter into the barn.

It is a simply glorious spring morning, Padah thought. She could hardly wait to see where he would lead them.

"Well, look at you, Nakeh!" the shepherd teased the young sheep. "You've nearly doubled in size. Your brother Zak better not miss a meal if he's going to keep pace with you now!"

Proudly, little Nakeh stood as straight and tall as possible, his small head erect in preparation for the customary loving pat from the master. Zak quickly ambled over, wasting no time in lining up for his turn.

The processional moved along as usual into the brisk morning air. This time, however, Zak checked out Zula's whereabouts before launching any unusual or challenging maneuvers. He had received from her more than one disapproving scowl and threatening grunt.

Once out on the open pasture, the shepherd slowly led his sheep down a hill. Rather than stopping along the way for a drink, the shepherd gently led them on through the deep meadows, knowing that the heavy morning dew was more than adequate to quench their thirst until midday.

When sweet and juicy herbs were out of the flock's reach, the shepherd would lift his arm and pluck off the tasty tidbits with his staff. Branches with high leaves and fruit he would break off for them. Rather than throw these morsels to the ground to be eaten, he held them behind him in his hand so that the sheep could nibble them as he walked in front.

Finally, having traveled a fair distance, the shepherd paused so that the sheep could lie down and rest in the shade. As Padah surveyed her surroundings, she stood captivated by its beauty. Numerous tall shade trees graced the banks of a lovely stream that curved and twisted its way through a picturesque valley. Hills sloped toward the stream covered with yellow buttercups and white lace flowers.

Padah turned and asked Joy, "Is this it? Did you know the shepherd would bring us here?"

"Yes, I knew but this is not what I meant when I said I had something special to show you," Joy responded with a smile.

"How could you possibly know where he was going to take us?" Padah inquired.

"After you have been with the shepherd for a while, Padah, and you choose to walk very close to his side, you cannot help but learn things about him," she explained. "You'll soon see what I mean, for the kind shepherd has somewhere very special that he goes and he will take you there if you wait for him at the meeting place. That is what I wanted to show you."

"Where is the meeting place?" Padah inquired.

"If you follow me I will take you to it. And if, after this, you choose to go there whenever he bids, I promise you, Padah, you will never be the same. Something incredibly wonderful happens that I cannot explain. It is there that the shepherd begins to change your heart and make you more like himself. He will reveal to you his desires and share with you great mysteries. Separating from the rest of the flock to follow him there may cost you acceptance from some of the others who do not choose to follow. You will become different, but you will also share a bond with those in the flock that have the same desire as you. They are the ones that frequent the meeting place."

Padah watched intently as the kind shepherd began to make his way down the hill. Eventually stopping beneath a grove of large shade trees, he turned around and stood gazing in the direction of the flock. With his rod and staff in hand, he began to call those that would come.

"He is ready, Padah. We must go now," instructed Joy.

Familiar with the well-worn path, Joy led Padah and her twins down the side of the hill to where the shepherd stood.

"Padah," the shepherd spoke softly, "I am so glad that you decided to come. I asked Joy if she would bring you with her today."

Turning around, the kind shepherd led his sheep to the edge of the stream. Following its course, both sheep and shepherd made their way toward the headwaters. It was here that the shepherd sat down to rest on a large flat rock along the edge next to his beloved sheep. From this location he could still see the rest of the flock on the hillside as well.

The fast-rushing waters cascaded over the mossy boulders, sparkling in the noontime sun like glass. Willow trees with their rich green branches hung over the edge of the stream where the birds seemed to extend their greeting, merrily chirping as they flitted from branch to branch. Padah's heart leapt in her chest, not from fear but from sheer delight.

The shepherd pointed to the source of the stream. "The water is purest at the headwaters, Padah."

Knowing that his sheep were frightened by the fast-running water and would not drink from it, even if it meant they could perish from thirst, the shepherd placed his rod and staff down in the water along the side of the stream. Carving out a sizeable channel by hollowing the earth below with the edge of his staff, the shepherd redirected some of the water into a small pool. Next he placed some of the surrounding rocks in a formation that would divert the flow of the stream. Here the shepherd's sheep drank deeply from the still waters.

Once the flock's thirst was sufficiently satisfied, the kind shepherd began to reveal to his sheep the most treasured secrets and longings of his own heart. Nothing satisfied him more completely than the times he spent with his sheep at the still waters. There remained, however, one unfulfilled desire of his heart.

If only, he wished, they would all come to the still waters.

"*The Lord is my shepherd; I have everything I need. He lets me rest in green meadows; He leads me beside peaceful streams. He renews my strength. He guides me along right paths, bringing honor to his name.*"

–Psalm 23:1-3 NLT

29

THE INVITATION

Enthralled by the beauty of her new surroundings, Padah failed to notice that both Grace and Melody were among the group.

"Grace!" Padah exclaimed. "I had no idea…" Her voice trailed off.

"Yes, I come here too."

"And Melody?" Padah asked. "Have you known about the still waters for a while too?"

"Oh yes! We come here as often as the shepherd calls us to the meeting place. Beautiful as the highlands of Menuca are, it is at the still waters that we are truly happiest and satisfied. There is nothing like them anywhere!"

"This is where the kind shepherd healed my broken heart," shared Grace.

"Yes!" Melody chimed in excitedly. "I used to be so overcome with fear sometimes that I did not know what to do. But when I came here with the kind shepherd, he taught me how to sing. Now when I am afraid in the night, I am able to sing his songs."

"It is a place of miracles, Padah," said Grace. "You can only come here with the shepherd. He is the one who creates the still waters. You will soon crave the deep waters and time with the shepherd as much as we do."

Looking at the radiance on both of their faces, Padah began to understand where Joy found the tranquility and calmness that made her so different from the other sheep. She had observed that there was something unique about both Grace and Melody too. Unlike Zula, Ursula, and some of the other sheep who were anxious, even hostile as they strove for a dominant position within the flock, Grace and Melody always seemed content. Padah admired their quiet strength, something that she herself wanted to possess.

Obviously pleased and enjoying his spot on the large flat rock, the shepherd removed his flute from his pocket and began to play softly. The soothing tones that floated out of the reed seemed to harmonize with the jubilant sound of the waterfall tumbling over the rocks. Settled peacefully at his feet, the sheep rested in the shade out of the heat from the afternoon sun, their eyes half closed as they silently ruminated. Captivated by the enchantment that surrounded her, Padah could not even think of closing her own eyes, for she was fascinated by the setting's loveliness and serenity. Inwardly she thought, I never want to leave this place!

With her mind occupied, Padah hardly noticed when the shepherd began speaking to her. Laying down the flute, he extended his right hand, his palm open in a welcoming gesture. In his left he held a sweet herb that he had just picked.

He spoke to her tenderly. "Come closer, Padah, and delight yourself in me, little one, for there is something very important in my heart that I would like to share with you."

Padah walked over to the shepherd, but it was he who reached down and lifted her into his arms. As he held her close to himself she felt the beat of his heart, his soft breath upon her head.

"Do you see the rest of the flock on the hills, Padah? Do you see the rest of my beautiful sheep?" the kind shepherd asked.

Padah's eyes obediently searched the hills behind her where the rest of the flock lay. Clustered in groups, there were hundreds of them upon the slopes, all ages, all sizes, some with young and some without.

"They were invited to the meeting place also, Padah," the shepherd continued. "You see, despite my love and desire for them, they do not share the same type of intimacy with me as the sheep at my feet. And although I would do anything for them, I cannot make them want to come."

Looking up into the kind shepherd's deep blue eyes, Padah thought she saw them begin to fill with tears.

"You see, they have learned to become content following after the other sheep rather than their shepherd," he said. "But the sheep at my feet, Padah, they are the ones that insist on drawing close. They are forever nuzzling their noses in my clothing in search of what I might have for them. The sheep at my feet have become so tame that they will allow me to pick them up without struggling to free themselves. They are the ones that long for the touch of my hand upon their heads. These same sheep are also the ones with whom I share the deep secrets of my heart. Before I rise to my feet, they are aware of my intent to move on. They have studied my ways and they know my thoughts. They are my precious treasure and I yearn for them even more than they yearn for the cool, still waters."

Without warning, a wind began to pick up and rattle the trees, scattering leaves and dust throughout the air. The once brilliant sun rapidly dimmed as large cumulous clouds overtook its face and stole its warmth.

Standing up, the shepherd readied the sheep at his feet to move downstream. Taking them to higher ground by way of a safe, much less difficult path, he led them to the protection of a rocky overhang where they could rest while the shepherd set out for the others on the hill.

Immediately he started summoning the sheep left behind on the slopes. For nearly half an hour, his shrill call echoed throughout the valley, but the sheep had dangerously distanced themselves from his presence and now failed to respond to his voice. Not only did the sheep appear to be indifferent to his call, but they also seemed entirely unaware that there had been any change in the weather. Patiently the shepherd continued to make his way up the slopes to retrieve them, calling them as he walked along.

By now the fluffy, white clouds had been replaced by dark, threatening thunderheads. The winds whistled and howled aggressively through the valley, causing small branches to fall from the trees as the dust storm intensified.

Swirling dirt flying into their eyes finally caught the sheep's attention. Startled by their sudden blindness, panic spread throughout the entire flock on the hill. Bleating and thrashing in confusion, they scrambled to their feet, running in the opposite direction from the shepherd.

Again he called out to them. Recognizing his rapidly approaching silhouette, they finally settled down. Once in their midst, the kind shepherd gathered them together, speaking gently as he started to lead them carefully down the hill to where the other sheep waited.

"Looks like a heavy storm tonight," he told them. "But we badly need the rain. Come now, we still have a bit of a journey before reaching the barn. You can rest safely there."

Pulling out his flute, he began to play. Joyfully the kind shepherd led all of his sheep home.

"I will be like a shepherd looking for his scattered flock.
I will find my sheep and rescue them from all the places to which
they were scattered on that dark and cloudy day.
Yes, I will give them good pastureland on the high hills.
There they will lie down in pleasant places
and feed in lush mountain pastures."
–Ezekiel 34:12-14 NLT

CHAPTER SEVEN

THE

TORM

The winds blew hard, the dark, brooding clouds continued to build, and the thunder rumbled across the highlands. Secure and content once again within the barn, the shepherd's flocks dozed. Although rain had not yet fallen on the hard, dry ground, the smell of it was not far off.

"Joy," Padah whispered softly, hoping to talk but not wanting to wake her friend if she had already fallen asleep.

"Yes?" Joy responded, still awake.

"Thank you for inviting me to the meeting place. I could never have imagined anything so perfect. We had a 'banquet,' a lavish meal with our shepherd, in more than one way at the stream, didn't we?" asked Padah. "He fed not only our stomachs but our hearts as well!"

"It was a banquet with our shepherd king!" Joy agreed.

"When do you suppose he'll take us there again?" Padah inquired.

"Very soon. The still waters is his favorite place too, and where I see him happiest. He will take us there as often as we ask, Padah," Joy affirmed.

Opening her mouth to ask Joy another question, Padah's words were swallowed up by an enormous boom of thunder. It was so loud neither Padah nor Joy noticed the sounds of the approaching townsmen. With eyes wide and ears erect, Padah stood trembling.

"Are you all right, Padah?"

"It's just that these storms remind me so much of the time when I broke my leg before the kind shepherd rescued me," Padah sighed, attempting to relax. Drawing Zak and Nakeh closer to herself, she whispered, "It's really okay. The storm will soon pass. You'll see." Padah spoke these words to encourage herself as well as her two little ones.

Again, a second wild streak of lightening forked across the sky. It initiated a crash of thunder that shook every rafter in the barn and awakened the shepherd within his cottage. Anticipating the frightened condition of his sheep, the kind shepherd rose to his feet. Quickly he opened the door of the cottage, while grasping for his lantern. As the shepherd passed through the breezeway that connected the house to the barn, he was immediately pelted by the fierce wind.

A bright flash briefly caught his attention. Mistaking it for a lightning strike, the shepherd did not see the torch in the hand of an intruder hiding around the corner.

"Hurry! He's on his way to the barn. It has to look like an act of God, a bolt of lightning," instructed one of the townsmen. "Quick! Light your torch with mine," he told another. "Can't take any chances it doesn't burn. The old man said to leave nothing standing!"

"Yeah, it's even better than we planned. He'll be in the barn with his precious sheep!" another one smirked.

Once the shepherd was inside, the four men moved rapidly to encircle the barn. As they poured fuel at the base of the structure, they eagerly awaited their opportunity.

"They'll see this one for miles!" one laughed.

"Yep. We'll have a real barbecue here. Anyone for lamb chops?" another joked. "Too bad there won't be anyone with water to help save him!"

Out of the sky surged a bolt of lightning so powerful that it toppled a tree several feet short of the barn. With the thunderous roar that followed, the leader of the group gave the signal.

In response to his motions, four torches sailed through the air, landing at once on the roof of the barn. Four more were ignited to kindle the base. Finished with their work and taking no time to admire the inferno they had just created, the strangers fled into the night, leaving behind them only the defenseless cries of the flock and their alarmed shepherd.

With flames licking at the corners of the roof, dark, acrid smoke billowed high into the evening sky. The heat from the fire escalated moment by moment, choking out the pure cool air. Dry grass around the perimeter swiftly burst into flames, engulfing the outside walls.

Thrusting open the doors of the smoke-filled barn, the shepherd labored desperately to move the sheep outside. In their frenzied state, however, they resisted him, bleating incessantly and shifting frantically, confused by their panic.

"This way! Come this way!" the shepherd agonizingly coaxed.

A large, fiery beam suddenly collapsed to the ground. With a tremendous crash, the barn's outside wall fell inward, dividing the sheep and separating Padah from her twins. And then she caught the scent of man, the one man she feared most.

"It's him! He has come to get me just as I expected. And this time he'll have my little ones as well!" she cried.

As a lightning bolt struck the corner of the house, the resounding crack of thunder was more than Padah could handle. Its familiar noise triggered such intense fear within her that, despite the gentle shepherd's attempt to reassure her, she bolted out of the barn into the darkness as fast as she was able to run.

Unaware of how long or how far she had run, Padah fought to catch her breath. The once elusive rain began to pour from the skies. Eagerly she searched for some sign of familiarity, but none could be found in the blackness of the night.

Not knowing what to do next or even in which direction to go, she wandered aimlessly, relentlessly, until her sore and exhausted body would go no further and demanded its sleep. Dropping to her knees

Padah hardly noticed when her frame hit the ground and her consciousness entered a state of slumber.

Deeply she slept throughout the remainder of the night only to awaken the next morning drenched by the cold rain and chilled all the way through. Disoriented, she tried desperately to recall the events of the previous evening. Where were her twins and the kind shepherd? Would he come for her? Where was the barn? So many unanswered questions, and rain, plenty of rain, more rain than she had seen since she came to live in the kind shepherd's pasture. When would it stop?

She had no idea that, only a couple of miles away, the kind shepherd also stood weary and alone amidst the rain-soaked smoldering ashes of what had once been the barn. Two charred beams lay on the ground. His beloved sheep were huddled together in frightened clusters. In shock they stood staring vacantly at their master. What did all this mean? they wondered.

Fortunately, the majority of the kind shepherd's sheep survived the previous night's holocaust. Joy, Zula, Ursula, Grace, Melody, Zak, and Nakeh were among those that remained.

Despite his sleepless night and broken heart, the kind shepherd's enduring strength and loving care of his sheep never faltered. They were, as always, his undeniable priority, his presence their only security.

With most of the sheep accounted for, the shepherd made plans to leave at once in search of Padah. Before doing so, he sought out one of the ewes.

"Grace," he asked lovingly, "Padah and I need your help right now. In her absence I can think of no one better to entrust her twins to than you. Will you nurse her babies and care for them as your own?"

Regrettably, until now, Grace had not been able to successfully carry a lamb to term. As with Padah, the trauma she had suffered while under the ownership of the old man had been severe. Dependable, adaptable, and a natural-born mother, Grace was the perfect choice. Her wonderful disposition and grateful manner toward the kind shepherd endeared her to him.

Upset by her friend's disappearance, Grace was not only willing but ready to assist. Only a few days prior, she had finally carried a pregnancy full term, only to give birth to a stillborn lamb, its small dead body cradled in the hands of the sad shepherd. Heavy with milk, she eagerly assumed her new maternal role with the guidance of the shepherd.

Grafting older orphaned twins to a different ewe was rarely successful, but the shepherd's patience and Grace's willingness to cooperate eventually worked. Bringing each lamb to her side one at a time, the shepherd assisted her with the nursing process. The scent of her fresh sweet milk attracted the very hungry lambs, and soon both Zak and Nakeh were suckling again, their small tails wagging and their stomachs swelling.

Delighted for her as much as the twins, the kind shepherd understood the emotional and physical ache experienced by Grace following her own grievous loss. And neither Zak nor Nakeh were yet old enough to survive apart from Padah. Such an adoption was necessary, temporary as it might be.

Having satisfied the needs of the rest of his flock, the kind shepherd ventured out in search of Padah.

"*Do not be afraid of the terrors of the night,*
nor fear the dangers of the day"...The Lord says,
"I will rescue those who love me. I will protect those who trust in my name.
When they call on me I will answer;
I will be with them in trouble. I will rescue them and honor them.
I will satisfy them with a long life and give them my salvation."
–Psalm 91:5, 14-16 NLT

FLOOD WATERS

Bewildered and forlorn, Padah stood listening to the rhythmic plunking of raindrops on the plants around her. In the dreary desolation of the early morning hours, she had only the foreboding whistling winds through the tall oaks overhead to keep her company. The discomfort from cold and hunger mattered little in comparison to the emptiness that engulfed her being, the separation from her twins and the shepherd's absence tearing her heart.

If only she hadn't run when the shepherd had called to her. If only she hadn't allowed fear to rule her. If only she'd trusted and listened to the shepherd, if only, she thought to herself, she would still be with all of them right now. She would not be alone.

Instead Padah found herself pummeled by the incessant rain, wandering in a dark gloomy forest that offered no hint of reprieve. She had no other choice but to continue alone in her search for a way home.

Without a path to follow, Padah slowly plodded and champed her way through the scrubby underbrush of the forest, as the rain continued to fall for several hours. Eventually reaching a clearing, she felt both relieved and encouraged. Hopefully she would find some sweet grass to nibble on or maybe even discover a clue to her whereabouts. She hated this loneliness and desperately hoped that the kind shepherd would soon find her.

Before long she became so engrossed in her mission of finding food, however, that she noticed little else. As she continued to chew her way along, the sound of rushing water caught Padah's attention, the same wonderfully refreshing sound she had enjoyed so much at the stream on that glorious afternoon with the kind shepherd. Surely if she could find her way to the stream again, he would be there along with the others. Yes, it was as simple as that, she decided. All she needed to do was find her way to the stream.

Lifting her head to catch a fresh scent, Padah's eyes slowly scanned the horizon. But the lingering mist continued to clutch at the marshy land that spread out before her, not allowing her to see what lay beyond. The beckoning noise was her only guide. With a heightened sense of anticipation, Padah set off in hopes of finding her shepherd at last.

Although making good time in his search, the kind shepherd remained a considerable distance from Padah. The continuous rain, now of tremendous concern, consumed his thoughts. The hard ground was not able to absorb all the rain that fell from the skies and very soon the stream would rise much too rapidly, spilling over its banks and flooding the land. Padah could easily be swept away to her death.

Finding a log nearby, the kind shepherd dropped to his knees in prayer.

"Dear Father," he prayed. "You alone understand how much I love this sheep. Padah has become my delight. I cannot bear to lose her. Take care of her in my absence. Comfort her and do not allow her to be harmed in any way. Please help me find her before it is too late."

Tears streamed down the kind shepherd's face, as he quietly wept at the thought of her being lost, alone, even dead. He missed her intensely.

Getting to his feet, the tenderhearted shepherd returned to his quest. His shrill call resounded through the forest.

Too distant to hear the voice of her shepherd, Padah continued in her determination to locate him. Due to her close proximity to the stream, she could hear nothing other than the water's deafening roar. Despite a fear of the fast-rushing current, her yearning for the shepherd was so great that even Padah's sense of caution was subdued. Perhaps I will find him at the water's edge, she told herself, remembering the time she had followed him to the still waters. Drawing closer to the stream's banks she searched frantically, continually, doggedly for him.

"He just has to be here somewhere," she lamented.

Her limp, much more pronounced from hours of walking, only gave her one more reason to question her value in the shepherd's eyes.

"Why would he depart from an entire flock to come after a cripple like me?" she asked herself. "Why wouldn't he leave me behind? It was I who left him this time. He already rescued me once. Maybe I've lost my chance forever. And now with the fire and the other sheep, what would ever make him come for me?" Padah fretted until she nearly convinced herself of her abandoned state.

With each passing hour her hopes diminished. Her heart sank deeper into despair, and she feared her pursuit was useless.

Her lonely desperate cry for her shepherd echoed across the valley but only the tall oaks could hear.

"Shepherd, I need you, I'm lost without you...don't leave me alone," she pleaded. "I need you to hold me, I can't live without you, I will certainly die without you! " she continued to cry out in anguish, until she could cry no longer.

The bank below Padah's small, thin legs regressed, as the hungry torrent ate away the stream's boundaries. Padah looked down just in time to see the edges of the bank disappear beneath her feet. The furious flood viciously swept her into its path, thrashing her downstream with such tremendous force that Padah was immediately consumed by its fury. Gasping for breath, terrified as never before, she realized that the end had come. She would never see the shepherd, her twins, or Joy again.

"Shepherd! Shepherd!" she cried out.

Raging waters finally sucked her into its depths. Helplessly she plunged beneath the surface, the force of the next wave dashing her foot and small head against a rock and knocking her completely unconscious. Her battered body sank slowly to the bottom of the stream.

Standing by its edge, two tall, male figures clothed in white garments watched the small sheep with compassion. Stepping into the flood's surging path, one of the strangers reached into the depths of the watery grave and lifted Padah's limp, water-soaked body from its grasp. With tenderness and mercy, his strong arms held her close before carrying her body up the slope away from the stream. He then gently laid her lifeless frame upon the grass. As the stranger leaned over her small body, he placed his hand upon her as he spoke to the other stranger by his side.

"Her time has not yet come," the first man said to the second. "She has much yet to learn; she will live and come to know his ways."

Padah's small body remained still. The two strangers continued on their way, and Padah would remember none of it.

"*When you go through deep waters*
and great trouble, I will be with you.
When you go through rivers of difficulty,
you will not drown!
When you walk through the fire of oppression,
you will not be burned up;
the flames will not consume you.
For I am the Lord your God,
the Holy One of Israel, your Savior."
–Isaiah 43:2 NLT

HILLS OF ENCHANTMENT

When Padah awoke the following morning, she did not recognize her surroundings nor remember what happened the night before. Her head throbbed so fiercely with pain that it was difficult to even think.

"I must remember what happened," she instructed herself. But the pounding in her head crowded out any memories.

Maybe things will make more sense once I have eaten, she thought to herself. Nagging questions penetrated her fog, and Padah's thoughts returned to the shepherd.

Will I ever find or see the kind shepherd again? What will become of me if he doesn't come? Nakeh and Zak, are they with him? Will I ever see my little ones again? Poor Padah could not imagine life apart from the kind shepherd. The thought haunted her unmercifully.

Hearing voices in the distance, she pricked her ears up to listen intently for a moment. Voices of strangers lingered in the air like a heavy fog. What could it possibly mean? she wondered to herself. Perhaps it was the shepherd, and he had brought someone to help him after all. But which direction did the voices come from? Straining to hear, hoping for further clues to decipher, Padah waited several minutes, but heard no more. She rose to her feet. I will find them now, she thought. He cannot be that far off.

Heading out in her search of her shepherd's whereabouts, Padah looked both up and down the stream. Which way is the right way? How could she be sure of knowing which way to turn? Failing to see any signs of him, Padah began to graze.

When she heard voices again, she looked up. She spotted in the distance land so lovely and so inviting that it could only belong to the kind shepherd. Perched on the top of a gentle slope sat a quaint and captivating structure. Padah had never seen the backside of the shepherd's home before. The lush grass behind the cottage sloped down to meet the valley below. It lay like a plush velvet carpet rolled out to welcome strangers. Thick green foliage and shrubbery framed the backside of the property and was now in full spring bloom. Bright pink, yellow and blue blossoms graced the shrub's branches in an explosion of color, complemented by abundant purple heather.

How absolutely glorious and inviting! she thought to herself. Padah could hardly wait to get home. Nearing the property, the welcome sound of the flock caused Padah's heart to skip with joy.

"I'm never going to run away again. No matter what happens, I will not ever leave the shepherd's side!" she promised herself.

As she approached the back of the residence, Padah could no longer restrain her joy but rather broke into a gallop. Moving rapidly, she hardly noticed the gully in her path. Attempting to avoid it, her legs slipped out from under her, causing Padah to tumble headlong into the ditch. Shocked by her sudden mishap and startled by a voice, she looked up at the hunched figure that now towered over her. The small, dark, piercing eyes, crooked nose, and sinister grin was alarmingly familiar.

And then, a horrifying thought entered Padah's mind. What if she had been deceived?

"So you've come back again for a visit, have you?" the old man sniveled. "How nice. How very nice, for me that is!" His nauseating laugh and gravelly voice sent chills through her.

"This can't be!" Padah shrieked. "This simply can't be!"

"Poor thing!" the old man sneered. "And you thought you were home again? Well you are!"

Shaking his threatening finger at her, the old man thrust his scrawny neck forward. Spitting his words into her face he declared, "You belong to me, remember? And this time you will not be rescued nor escape!"

Grabbing hold of her wool, the old man pulled her from the ditch and forced her to her feet. While he kicked open the gate, he abruptly shoved Padah into what appeared to be his back yard. In utter dismay she recognized Mara and countless other sheep that had inexplicably disappeared from the kind shepherd's pasture over time.

He has done this, Padah thought to herself. The old man is the one who has been doing all the stealing while accusing the kind shepherd of his own deceitful deeds. What a pitiable and confused group they were compared to the sheep of the kind shepherd's flock.

She nearly forgot how much the shepherd had changed her life, how great his mercy, until now. Deeply touched, Padah could not quell the aching pain she felt for the others. Their hopeless state was nearly intolerable. Padah no longer hurt just for herself.

Somehow, she thought, they must find their way back home, for they need the shepherd as desperately as I do. They have no other hope.

Mara's voice interrupted her thoughts. "So you fell into the old man's trap and now you are back where you started," she spat.

Padah shook her head. "I never would have guessed the gorgeous flowering shrubs and magnificent lush green slopes at the back of the property belonged to the old man. It looked so beautiful from the stream." Padah gazed at Mara in disbelief. " I felt anything that lovely must belong to the kind shepherd. Instead, the old man used it as a ploy. It was nothing more than a trap!"

"Yes," agreed Mara with knowing eyes, "but why should you wander way over here?"

"There was an absolutely dreadful fire!" Padah answered in despair. "The kind shepherd's barn was struck by lightning during that ferocious storm and I'm afraid his barn may have burnt down."

"And?" Mara prodded.

"And when I picked up the scent of man during the fire and heard the most horrendous crack of thunder, I ran in fear thinking the old man had come after me. I became lost and separated from the rest of the flock."

"Oh," Mara lowered her voice, "that is dreadful! And most unfortunate, I might add, as it is almost certain that you will never get out of here now. But then, let's face it," she added. "You never really belonged there anyway. You are one of us. No better, no worse, and your fate just the same as ours, no matter how much you want to stretch your imagination!"

With little left to be gained in continuing in their conversation, Padah stood silently by her friend. Mara didn't understand the kind shepherd or his ways at all, she told herself. The ropes of her own disappointment undeniably bound her. Padah's only hope was that, with time, Mara would experience the shepherd's kindness for herself.

Sauntering slowly over to join in their conversation, Mara's friend Huldah spoke.

"Seems we have another visitor to our valley. Guess the shepherd on the hill can't keep hold of his sheep, no matter how much stealing he resorts to. You'd think with all the water he has there'd be some sense of loyalty or contentment up there!" she sniped.

Padah looked at her in disbelief. "How could you ever say such a thing?" she cried incredulously. "That is completely untrue. He has never stolen anyone's sheep!"

"Oh, is that so? Why, then, do his flocks continue to grow and his sheep have so much more to eat and drink than the rest of us down here in the valley? Evidently your friend, Mara, hasn't been listening to what the men in the valley have discovered. Not only has the shepherd's flocks grown, but he's moved the property lines in order to water and feed them, while the rest of us continue to suffer!"

Padah stood absolutely stunned. She couldn't even open her mouth to speak as Huldah rambled on with her barnyard gossip.

"As I understand, it wasn't mere coincidence that the shepherd's barn burnt to the ground the other night! From what I've heard of the men talking to the old man, it won't be the last big blaze on his property either. Next time none of his sheep will escape alive! Very soon they're planning to go back to finish the job they began the night of the storm and run him out of town for good. Guess it's been an ongoing battle between the shepherd and the old man for years!"

Unable to keep silent any longer, Padah corrected Huldah's perception.

"I used to live here among the flocks with the rest of you, until one day the old man drove the flocks so hard I fell. I lay there with a broken leg, nearly trampled to death by the rest of the herd. The old man left me to die. Had not the kind shepherd taken me to the highlands and nursed me back to health, I most certainly would have died. It is you who do not know nor understand his ways. He is not what you say. Your death is as certain as mine if you continue to close your eyes and ears to the truth. The kind shepherd will come for me again, you'll see, and for you too, if you choose to go. It is the old man who's controlling this valley through fear and lies. He is the one who cannot be trusted."

"That is easy for you to say now. Your life has been soft! You have nothing to tell us until you have endured what we have!" Huldah spewed hatefully.

With that Huldah and Mara walked off, leaving Padah alone to face her own unresolved questions.

Did the kind shepherd know where she was at this moment? Was he still mindful of her? What was to become of her after all...and her twins? What if he really didn't return for her this time?

Padah thought about the day the shepherd had notched her ear. How could she forget the look in his eyes as he held her? Their depth...their warmth...their honesty. There was an unmistakable and engulfing love so powerful she could never forget. He had marked her as his own, but more than that he had claimed a place within her heart. Yes, the kind shepherd would come for her, Padah decided. Nothing could hold him back.

"O Lord, you have searched me
and you know me.
You know when I sit and when I rise;
you perceive my thoughts from afar.
You discern my going out and my lying down;
you are familiar with all my ways.
Before a word is on my tongue you know it
completely, O Lord.

You hem me in—behind and before;
you have laid your hand upon me.
Such knowledge is too wonderful for me,
too lofty for me to attain.
Where can I go from your Spirit?
Where can I flee from your presence?
If I go up to the heavens, you are there;
if I make my bed in the depths, you are there.
If I rise on the wings of the dawn,
if I settle on the far side of the sea,
even there your hand will guide me,
your right hand will guide me,
your right hand will hold me fast.
If I say, "Surely the darkness will hide me and the
light become night around me,"
even the darkness will not be dark to you;
the night will shine like the day,
for darkness is as light to you.
How precious to me are your thoughts, O God!
How vast is the sum of them!"
–Psalm 139:1-12,17 NIV

CHAPTER TEN

THE VALLEY OF
*A*CHOR

When evening descended upon the Valley of Achor, it ushered in an eerie and imposing darkness that Padah had not felt for a long time. Even during the dark, lonely nights on her journey to find the shepherd, she had not experienced the depth of fear and despair that was present here. The Valley of Achor, whose name literally meant "the valley of troubling," was a place of unparalleled sorrow. Tragically for those that knew nothing else, it had become a way of life unquestioned as well.

Spotting Mara near the fence, Padah walked over to where she stood.

"With night closing in, the old man will soon come to take us back to the barn," Padah said.

"Maybe, maybe not," Mara responded.

"Surely he won't leave us out here to be prey for the wild dogs, coyotes, or whatever else decides to come along," Padah objected.

"Wouldn't be the first time," Mara told her. "And certainly wouldn't be the last! The old man has gotten very careless with his flocks since you were here last. He spends more time in town than he does at home caring after his sheep!"

Refusing to be left out, and desirous of appearing knowledgeable herself, Huldah sidled up to Mara and bellowed, "Yep, I remember clearly one particular night when almost three hundred sheep were savagely killed by a couple of wild dogs, just rampant slaughter, I tell you! All because of neglect!"

"Looks like another night on our feet," Mara added resignedly. "No one can possibly rest when there's that kind of threat."

Fortunately, at that moment, the old man walked briskly toward them. Opening the rickety gate, he yelled, "Move! Get going! Back to the barn all of you!"

As he cracked his stick loudly, the flock began to bleat and crowd together, skittering in the direction of the barn. Thankful that Mara's prediction did not come to pass, Padah could hardly wait for a much-needed night of rest. Once in the barn she settled down into a corner next to Mara, where she quickly fell into a deep sleep and did not stir until morning.

Awakened by the brilliant sunrise, Padah felt renewed hope that today the kind shepherd would arrive to take her home. Filled with enthusiasm despite her surroundings, she looked for Mara and Huldah, already on their feet and heading out of the barn together in search of food.

"Wait for me!" Padah cried out, hurrying to catch up. Reaching their side she chirped, "Isn't this an incredible spring day?"

"What's incredible is that we're still alive in this place to experience it!" rebuked Huldah.

Saddened by their continual state of discouragement, Padah attempted to console them. "I can't imagine how difficult and depressing your life has been here. It's even worse than I remember it. Just the same, I can't stand by and watch you live out your days without any hope. Life with the kind shepherd is very different from what you have here. And—"

Cutting her short, Huldah mimicked, "Life with the kind shepherd! Life with the kind shepherd! That is all we ever hear from you! If your life with the kind shepherd was so grand, why did you run away?

Where is your kind shepherd now? Whose eyes do you think you're pulling the wool over any way? Your own?"

"I only wanted to—"

"You only wanted to what? Flaunt your temporary good fortune? Leave us alone, Padah. We're tired of fairy tales!"

Leaving her behind again, the two disgruntled sheep turned away to talk between themselves on their path to the pasture. Stunned by their criticism, Padah stood speechless and dejected.

"Don't pay any attention to their biting remarks," she heard someone say behind her. Abruptly turning her head to catch sight of who was speaking, Padah noticed a very pregnant sheep. "They both have had some very unpleasant experiences and find comfort in licking one another's wounds." she smiled at Padah. "My name is Eve. I wouldn't mind hearing more about the kind shepherd. That is, if you still want to talk about him."

"Of course," Padah responded gratefully, covering her pain and disappointment at being scorned. She returned Eve's smile, happy for the chance to make a new friend. "How long have you been here?"

"About a year. As you can see, I am due to lamb in a few weeks. I can hardly wait. It will be my first season!"

"How exciting for you, Eve!"

"Do you have any of your own?"

"I bore twins just a few weeks ago. They were my first as well. I miss them both terribly, and if I were not confident that they were safely in the kind shepherd's care right now, I could not stand it!"

"What was it like, giving birth I mean?"

"Oh, it's difficult at first, and there can certainly be complications, but it's worth all the hard work at the end. The kind shepherd never left my side. He held my head in his hand, encouraging me the entire time. Had he not been there, surely one of my twins would have died. The kind shepherd breathed life back into him!"

"How dreadful! What are they like now?" Eve inquired.

"Well, Zak, rather Zachar, my firstborn, is the strong and adventurous one! His name means 'to remember.' He reminds me of the kind shepherd's faithfulness. Sometimes I fear that if it were possible, Zak would be capable of testing even the kind shepherd's patience, he has such energy and enthusiasm for life and is continually overstepping the boundaries. He is my fearless clown."

"Unlike Zak, Nakeh, his brother, has struggled from the very beginning. His name means 'contrite and dejected,' for he's the one that reminds me of the shepherd's great mercy. While admiring his older brother's courage and liveliness, Nakeh has always lagged behind, pressing in to my side because of his need. Fortunately, he has developed a great fondness for the kind shepherd as well, and follows him nearly everywhere. He's a bit self-conscious because of his physical weakness and strange black spot, but he has a soft heart and strong desire to do what is right. My twins are as different as summer and winter. I cannot wait to be reunited with them again!"

"I'm glad you're here in time for my delivery, Padah. I've felt so alone for so long and, I must admit, very anxious a great deal of the time. My heart has yearned for someone whom I could trust and talk to. There is another sheep who's also very new to the flock and spends a lot of time alone as well."

"Which one is she?" Padah asked, craning her neck to survey the flock.

"The speckled one, over there in the corner. It must be the color of her coat that the rest of the sheep object to. With so much uncertainty and suspicion in this valley, anyone different or anything unusual seems to be rejected."

"Then it appears we could all three benefit from becoming friends!" Padah cheerfully concluded. "Let's go introduce ourselves."

Despite her heavily protruding belly, Eve kept pace with Padah as they ambled across the barnyard together. Taking note of their approach, the speckled sheep lifted her eyes in bewildered interest, her fixed gaze conveying mistrust.

"Would you mind if we joined you?" Eve inquired, her winsome smile dismantling the young sheep's guard.

Noticing the metal tub of water next to the speckled sheep, Eve continued, "We're a bit thirsty and thought you might want to join us in our walk out to the pasture afterward."

"I would like that," the small sheep replied.

"My name is Eve, and this is my new friend, Padah."

"Hello, my name is Hope."

"Well then, Padah, let's have a drink of water before we head for the pasture," Eve urged.

"Great idea! But where is the drinking water?"

"Here, right in front of you, in the metal tub of course!" Eve giggled rolling her eyes as if to suggest Padah was joking.

Staring into the polluted water with dead insects floating on top, Padah nearly lost her breakfast.

"Is there something wrong, Padah?" Eve probed.

"Is there another place to drink from?"

"Not unless you want to quench your thirst at the parasite-infested potholes, where the flocks have relieved themselves and tramped through. Some of the sheep have become so sick from drinking the foul water that it drew the life right out of them. Others had to be put down later!"

"I think I'll wait a bit longer."

If only Eve knew what it had been like in the kind shepherd's pasture, thought Padah. But if I tell her now it will only add to her disappointment. At the right time, I'll share with her the truth and she will eventually desire to be with the kind shepherd as much as I do.

"I will give them a heart to know me, that I am the Lord.
They will be my people, and I will be their God,
for they will return to me with all their heart."

–Jeremiah 24:7 NIV

MARA

Despite Mara's stoic attempt at appearing courageous, Padah knew that deep inside, pain festered. Huldah, who professed loyalty to Mara, did nothing to lessen her friend's sorrow.

Across the paddock, Mara stood alone. Observing her, Padah decided to extend herself once again. She walked over and gently nudged her shoulder.

"Mara, how long have you actually lived in the valley?"

"Long enough to know that some things will never change and you're better off not continually stirring things up!"

"That was never my intent, Mara. You of all sheep must know that about me. It was you who helped take care of me in my youth while here in the valley. You know more about my past than I do. I have always considered you my friend. All I wanted was for you to have the same chance for happiness that I had been given."

"That is not possible, especially at this stage in my life. I will never escape this place. I was doing fairly well at accepting that until you came along. At least I have learned to become content in my old age!"

"But that is my point, Mara. You still have many years left, and if you choose to settle for nothing more than this, you will not be around in your old age!"

"What makes you suddenly so knowledgeable?"

"The kind shepherd, Mara. If you ever dare to look deep into his eyes to accept his invitation to go with him to the meeting place, you will know what I mean. No one else can tell you what it's really like. It's an experience that will change you forever. But you must choose to do it for yourself. No one can make you go and you cannot afford to let anyone hold you back.

"I now belong to the kind shepherd. Take a look at my ear, Mara. Do you see his mark? At first I was afraid of his mark. I knew it would hurt for him to place it on me, and I was not sure I wanted it. But now I find it to be beautiful, because it represents hope, a constant reminder that I am his responsibility. Yes, it is true, I am nothing more than a defenseless sheep, but I am his sheep and because of that I know he will come for me. Oh, Mara, please say you'll come with us too!"

Suddenly, a clue to Mara's apprehension occurred to Padah.

"Mara, are you afraid that you are not good enough to be one of the sheep in the kind shepherd's flock? Do you fear his rejection? Are you wondering if he chose Zula over you?"

"Well, wouldn't you?" Mara snapped.

Padah sighed. "Yes, I suppose I would feel inadequate as well after everything that happened. Sometimes I feel that way about my limp. My deformity and my obvious lack of perfection is visible for everyone to see. Other sheep question my value, often suggesting it is I who did something to cause my condition. I do understand, Mara, and what's more important, is that the kind shepherd understands, more than you think. He is teaching me that the shame is not in my weakness, but rather my unwillingness to trust him in times of need. That is how I ended up back here. I allowed fear rather than trust to determine my course."

Padah looked at her friend with affection. "Mara, why did you cut yourself off from the other sheep in the kind shepherd's pasture, but did not do the same with me?"

"You have always been different from the others, Padah."

"Different in what way?"

"Well, you never rejected me or acted unsympathetic to my suffering. You haven't forgotten where you came from. Maybe there is a bond because I was there when you were born to share in your humble beginnings."

"You were with me when I was born?"

"Indeed I was! You had a real hard time at first. Your mother died giving birth to you. Joy and I witnessed the whole horrifying event. And then, unlike other orphans, you refused to even take a bottle, not that the old man seemed to care much, he had so many other sheep to tend to. Little thing that you were, you nearly starved to death until Joy began to nurse you. She couldn't stand to see you wither away. You would have thought she was the mother. You two have stuck together ever since!"

Completely caught off guard, Padah was speechless. No wonder she and Joy shared such a special closeness. It never occurred to her. Had it not been for both Joy and the kind shepherd, Padah would never have survived.

"I am so glad that you shared that with me, surprising as it is, Mara. I guess we never fully realize what we have been saved from, do we? I want you to know that I am very thankful you are my friend. We would all feel a terrible loss if anything ever happened to you."

Although difficult for Mara to acknowledge outwardly, Padah's unconditional love for her friend was becoming an irresistible force. Healing within Mara's heart was slowly taking place. The walls were crumbling.

"Thank you, Padah."

Together they sauntered across the field which divided the old man's property from the kind shepherd's. Padah gazed through the rusty, woven wires to the lush green fields just beyond. Realizing she was now the one on the opposite side of the fence from the shepherd's property, Padah's heart sank, like a once buoyant balloon that had lost all its air. This, she thought to herself, is the very same place Mara stood so many times in the past, despondent and depressed, as I walked by with the shepherd. The devastating reality was indescribable. For the first time she was beginning to understand.

"It's amazing how one's perspective can change so quickly, isn't it?" Padah sighed. "I'm so sorry I never really understood."

Continuing to stand at the fence, Padah allowed herself time to reflect on the events of the day. So much had been revealed during her conversation with Mara. And now, though she desperately wanted to leave the Valley of Achor, her desire to help Mara deepened. Padah began to feel a new sense of her own destiny. Could she do less for these unhappy sheep than was done for her by Joy and the kind shepherd?

Maybe this is what Joy meant when she said, "There is a fate worse than ending up in the old man's pasture." Could that awful fate be not having the chance to ever know the depth of love possible with the kind shepherd? Was it never once drinking deeply of the refreshing still waters found only at the meeting place, nor feeling the euphoric peace and pleasure of his embrace?

Padah remained deep in thought for quite some time as Mara nibbled at the sparse, course grass along the fence. It was too much to take in all at once, she decided. However, one truth remained obvious. She must find a way to get at least Mara out.

"This time, I will not leave without her," Padah vowed.

For I know the plans I have for you,"says the Lord. "They are plans for good and not for disaster, to give you a future and a hope. In those days when you pray, I will listen. If you look for me in earnest, you will find me when you seek me. I will be found by you," says the Lord. "I will end your captivity and restore your fortunes. I will gather you out of the nations where I sent you and bring you home again to your own land."

–Jeremiah 29:11,12 NLT

NIGHT *of* VISITORS

Once again night fell upon the Valley of Achor, spreading its ominous blanket of darkness. Unlike the previous night, the old man did not walk out to the pasture and lead his flocks into the barn for safety. Instead, he remained in town, devising plans for his next assault upon the kind shepherd and his unsuspecting flock.

The town hall was filled to overflowing on this particular night. Rumors of the kind shepherd's conspiracy to cut off water supplies in order to gain the allegiance of the local residents had prompted their meeting. Known to them as the highland shepherd, his presumed self-serving reputation had ignited tempers and fostered resentment.

Commanding the community's rapt attention, the old man stepped up to the podium. His slumped silhouette and dirty, disheveled appearance was hardly noticed as he delivered his fiery depiction of a calculating and heartless highland shepherd.

"There is no time to waste, I tell you. Every minute that passes is one more minute in the hands of this malicious neighbor who seeks only to undermine the inhabitants of this community while serving his own best interests! I myself have seen him move the property lines, cutting off the only source of irrigation, denying water to all but his own flocks! He is both a liar and a thief! And he is conniving! To gain your sympathy as well as those of local farmers, he even set his own barn on fire last week. He is a cheat and a butcher who would sell your sheep for his own profit before ever touching one of his own. I ask you again. Where do you think your lost sheep have gone? Who is the fool in this situation, the highland shepherd or the residents of this community? If we do not put an end to his debauchery and deceit soon, it will be too late and we will have no one to blame but ourselves!"

Amid loud shouts of agreement and a burst of thunderous applause, the old man stepped down from his post of authority. Congregating around him, the agitated men in the crowd soon formed an alliance and began to plot a scheme to extinguish their assumed enemy.

While the meeting that night continued for several hours, the confused sheep back at the old man's farm stood on their weary feet. Anxious and afraid, they could not settle down nor rest, hoping that the old man would soon return. But instead of the anticipated gravelly voice of their master, they heard the distant yip of coyotes and the howl of neighboring dogs.

"I hate nights like this!" Eve lamented. "It is impossible to rest. The kind shepherd would never have left us out here knowing we are unable to fend for ourselves, would he?"

"No!" Padah affirmed. "He would risk his own life before endangering ours. There were times he would not even lie down to sleep for an entire night so that he could care for us." Then, hoping to divert their fears, Padah asked, "Eve, you never told me how you became part of the old man's flock."

"Oh, I too once lived on the highlands with the rest of the kind shepherd's sheep, but I was afraid to become earmarked. When the day came for the kind shepherd to mark me, I hid in fear. I went down into a cove, where I nestled into the soft ground. I was very comfortable for a while, but when I finally decided to return, I couldn't get up. I rolled backwards with my legs thrashing in the air."

"You ended up cast?"

"Yes! I was cast down on my back, completely unable to right myself. Soon the buzzards began to gather overhead and I thought it would surely be the end of me. The harder I tried to kick myself free, the worse my situation got, until finally I could no longer feel my legs and air filled my stomach, signaling death was not far off. I lay there filled with despair. I longed for the good shepherd to find me. But before he could do so, the old man snatched me up and took me away! He spared me from death. But in exchange for my life, I became his prisoner."

"How utterly frightful!" Padah sympathized. "Did you ever think of escaping from here?"

"I thought about it all the time at first. But now, being heavy with lamb, it would be impossible for me to leave. At least there is food, water, and companionship with the rest of the flock. I think of it less and less now. I have become accustomed to life here. Believe it or not, it's not that bad once you get used to things."

"Accustomed to this? You live a life of fear and neglect. How could you ever get accustomed to that? If not for yourself, Eve, don't you worry about raising lambs in a place like this?"

"I don't feel I really have a choice. Sometimes you just can't go back."

"But I thought you said you wanted to hear more about the kind shepherd and his ways."

"I want to. I really do, Padah. I wish I knew him like you do. I wish I had the same confidence that you have in him. But as much as I'd like for things to be different, it's just not that easy for me. At least here I know what to expect. Especially now with the delivery so close, the thought of change is overwhelming. I don't know if I could begin all over again. I'm sure it's a hard thing for you to understand, but there are things that I would lose as well. Anyway, you seem so much more adventurous and courageous than I am."

Padah's heart sank once again in disappointment. Despite their deplorable circumstances, her new friends appeared to fear change more than they feared their uncertain destiny or present situation, more than they wanted to be free. The entire valley and its unwary inhabitants were helplessly entranced in a deception they didn't even seem to question.

Choosing to forget her dismal surroundings for the moment, Padah noticed that it was still a beautiful spring night, even in the old man's pasture. If only the kind shepherd were close by, it would be an absolutely perfect evening! she thought to herself. She could be with him nearly anywhere and be happy.

The full moon glowed brightly and the sweet scent of magnolia trees near the old man's house lingered, intoxicatingly fragrant. The soft swooshing sounds of their branches filled the warm night air, testifying once again that springtime flourished with all its wonder, newness, and promise of hope, a hope tragically overlooked by the sheep in the old man's pasture.

Mara and Huldah strolled over to Padah and Eve.

"We better stick close together tonight," Mara said, her tone of voice unmistakably serious.

"We won't be going anywhere at this late hour. With a full moon we are that much easier for predators to spot. We could end up with only half the flock left by morning!" said Huldah.

The grim reality of her words hardly settled in when the sound of helpless shrieks startled them all. A ewe standing alone at the edge of the pasture was an easy target for a group of unwelcome coyotes. Although attempting to break free from their grasp, she helplessly collapsed to the ground. Hungrily they gnawed at her neck until seconds later, she lay dead, her thin neck broken.

"Oh, Padah, where is he? Why doesn't the old man come home?" Eve cried. "Surely the coyotes will slaughter us all before he returns!"

Bleating frantically, the horrified flock began to scatter in different directions. Eve, fearing separation during their flight, tried to remain alongside Padah. The coyotes circled the perimeter of the pasture, hemming in the defenseless flock to further prevent escape, calculating their next assault.

"Please, stay close to me," Eve begged. "I am so afraid. I cannot run as fast with my baby!"

Breathless and panicked herself, Padah pressed into Eve's side.

"I'm here, right beside you. Try to get into the center of the flock! Now, Eve, push now!"

The pack of coyotes continued their ruthless slaughter. One by one the unsuspecting sheep were chased and driven senseless by their predators. Spotting an advancing coyote, Padah feared for Eve's safety, knowing her pregnancy made her an easy victim.

"Get out of my way, Eve! Give room to those of us who have the best chance of survival," Huldah charged. "Don't be so selfish!"

Shoving Eve to the outside, Huldah closed rank, leaving Eve isolated and unprotected from the rest of the flock.

Quickly a coyote advanced in an effort to take advantage of its unguarded prey. Although racing as fast as she was able, Eve could no longer keep up. She had exerted herself beyond her limits to endure. Water gushed down her legs, followed by her own warm blood.

"Look!" Padah cried out to Mara. "Poor Eve is slipping her young! We must get to her right away!"

Forgetting their own danger for the moment, both Mara and Padah ran toward Eve, who was by now close to dropping to the ground in utter hysteria, continuing to hemorrhage.

"We're here, Eve!" Padah reassured her.

Suddenly, the threatening growl of the coyote behind them made the three turn. As they stared into the glaring, brazen eyes and snarling face of their adversary, three more advanced toward them. Slow but calculating, the four coyotes pressed in upon the three sheep, who stood paralyzed and powerless, quaking in fear.

It can't end this way without the shepherd, Padah thought to herself. He has always come for me when I needed him. If he doesn't come now, not only will we all die, but whatever will become of my twins?

In a desperate lament for help, Padah's shrill wail for her shepherd penetrated the heavens.

With a sudden yelp as though they'd been stuck, the four coyotes, tails between their legs, scuttled into the darkness. The three bewildered sheep watched in disbelief.

Unaware of the imposing presence of three white-robed figures behind them, Padah, Mara, and Eve continued to stand, wondering why they had been spared when so many of the flock lay dead.

"Oh Padah! It has happened again! I have failed to carry another pregnancy to term," Eve sobbed. "I don't think I can possibly bear the pain and disappointment any longer. It would have been best if the coyotes had finished me off with the others. At least this endless cycle of pain would be over with, once and for all!"

Padah moved closer to her friend. "Eve, I'm so sorry. I don't know what I can possibly say to lessen your sorrow, except that I would have felt a terrible loss with your death."

"But look at me now, Padah!"

"I know. If only I could have done something more to help you. I am so sorry, Eve."

"Where is the kind shepherd?" Eve sobbed. "If only he had been here!"

"I don't know, Eve. There are so many things I don't have answers for myself and really only one thing I know for certain. The longer I'm apart from the shepherd, the more I realize how much I desperately need him and how little I am able to do for myself. We are defenseless sheep who, without the kind shepherd, have no hope!"

"Hope? Who in this place can have hope?" Eve screeched. "The old man will most assuredly send me to the butcher. He threatened to finish me off after I slipped my last lamb. He will have no mercy this time and surely no reason to keep me. I am of no value to him or anyone. And, I bear the scorn of most of the flock. Even they look at me with disgust! Padah, you did me no favor in attempting to save my life!" Eve began to weep.

"Well, you and I both know, you do not really belong to the old man anyway. You were part of the kind shepherd's flock long before the old man stole you," Padah gently encouraged.

But Eve shook her head. "It was the kind shepherd that gave me my name and declared my purpose! I was meant to be a giver of life, yet I fail to fulfill my destiny. That is all I have ever wanted. Even the kind shepherd will eventually find displeasure in me."

Gazing across the field, Padah silently pondered Eve's words for several minutes before speaking. "As defenseless sheep, we are dependent upon our master. And that is what gives the kind shepherd real joy. We are his delight and ultimately his responsibility. It is only upon the highlands, in service to the kind shepherd, that your deepest desires can ever be satisfied! Won't you come with us, Eve, when he returns? You are my friend and I do not want to risk losing you a second time."

"But how can you know for sure that he will come?"

"He has never failed me," Padah smiled softly. "As I see it, you have no other choice. He is your only hope."

"Because he loves me," says the Lord,
"I will rescue him;
I will protect him, for he acknowledges my name.
He will call upon me, and I will answer him in trouble,
I will deliver him and honor him.
With long life will I satisfy him
and show him my salvation."
—Psalm 91:14,15 NIV

CHAPTER THIRTEEN

RYLANDS
OF DESPAIR

The old man's euphoric sense of victory quickly faded upon his return home. The reality of his losses out in the pasture became all too apparent. Fifty-one mangled sheep lay dead as a reminder of his reckless neglect. Of the sheep that remained, the majority stood motionless in a state of shock.

Eve wept quietly, mourning the loss of her baby ram, as Padah and Mara comforted her. Though she had sustained few injuries during the raid, Huldah nursed her hurts off in a corner of the pasture by herself.

"She'll have to find someone else to befriend," Mara said, glancing at Huldah with disgust. "I can't believe what she did to Eve!"

"She'll lose the only friend she has in the flock if she loses you," Padah observed.

"I can't help it. She reminds me too much of Zula now that I understand how she works." Mara looked at Padah questioningly. "Do you think there's any hope for her?"

"There's always hope, but until she recognizes her ways and sees her own lack, there is little incentive to change."

The old man raised his raspy voice, instructing the sheep to follow him back into the barn for the night. The herd followed silently, tired but relieved to leave the darkness behind.

71

Flanked by Mara and Padah, Eve had just settled down onto the ground, when the old man walked briskly toward them. Impatiently he took hold of Eve's neck and yanked her up.

"So, you lost my new lamb did you?" he spat in her face. "I thought it was yours!" Without bothering to examine Eve's injuries, the old man threw her down and stomped out of the barn. For Eve, sad and scared, but angry too, this was the defining moment.

"I will be going with you when the kind shepherd comes!" she choked.

Saying nothing more, Eve closed her eyes, as if to shut out her anguished thoughts. The rest of the flock followed suit, with not so much as a bleat heard for the rest of the night.

The stillness of the night could not quiet the longing in Padah's heart. She missed the shepherd terribly. Even her special friendship with Eve and Mara could not compare to the bond she shared with her shepherd. Nothing was more deeply satisfying to her soul, no communion so sweet, as what she experienced with him. Only the anticipation of his return kept Padah going. Closing her eyes once again, she tried to recapture the memories. They led her into the most pleasurable rest she had enjoyed since their separation.

When morning came, the events of the horrifying night before seemed but a bad dream. Padah found it difficult to believe they had transpired. No true shepherd would have neglected his flock that way, she told herself. But with so many sheep absent, and ill-fated Eve no longer pregnant, the sad truth could not be denied.

Without warning, a sudden dizziness swept over Padah. Her knees buckled and her legs splayed out to each side, as she fought to keep from falling. I need more sleep, she thought to herself. I have felt so tired these last few days.

Walking over to the fence that bordered the old man's property, Padah lay down in the sparse dry grass for some rest. Eve soon joined her friend.

"Are you all right, Padah? You didn't eat with the rest of us this morning. That's not like you!"

"I know. I'm just a little tired and not too hungry."

With eyes focused upon the distant highlands well beyond their reach, the two sheep sat quietly, each thinking upon their uncertain future, each mourning losses too deep for words to express.

In spite of all her attempts to encourage herself and the other sheep, Padah feared she might not escape the old man's pastures as easily as she hoped. Her strength had ebbed. The small cough she had developed from her long wet night after the storm had now been replaced with heaviness in her chest, making breathing difficult.

I am not even certain that I would have strength enough to leave, Padah thought to herself, self-doubt once again plaguing her. What if the kind shepherd never finds me, or worse yet, if he finds me less than acceptable by now?

Unexpectedly her thoughts were interrupted by a familiar voice.

"Padah! Where ever have you been?"

Lifting her head up, Padah could hardly believe her eyes. Joy stood just on the other side of the old fence.

"Joy, oh, Joy! I can't believe it's you. I wondered if I would ever see you again!"

"I know," Joy agreed.

"This is my new friend, Eve," Padah added.

"Hello, Eve. I'm so glad to know Padah has not been alone," Joy responded, smiling warmly. "Just the same, the kind shepherd has been searching for you everywhere! There has been such sadness in his eyes, Padah. Each time he returned without finding you, his sorrow would deepen. We have all missed you!"

"I have missed you, too, and the time I have spent apart from the shepherd has been absolutely miserable. You cannot imagine the horrors we have had to endure here! Tell me about Zak and Nakeh. Are they all right?"

"Yes, they're fine. Grace is taking good care of them for you, though they miss you terribly. But, tell me, what caused you to end up here?"

"Fear! Oh, Joy, you know how that has always been such struggle for me! It could be my undoing now if the kind shepherd does not rescue me soon. When that terrible storm passed over the highlands and ravaged the kind shepherd's barn, I lost my head. I feared the old man had come for me. All I could think of was to run. Now I've lost the only place of true peace and happiness I had ever known. I'm so unhappy. Even my confidence in the shepherd's return for me is weakening. I have told everyone else about his faithfulness, but deep inside I am barely able to hold on myself!"

"Padah, we each have shadows from our past, places within us that need healing. These are our weaknesses, and if we do not face them, they can drive us beyond all reason. It is in those times of unwelcome loneliness and separation, when we so desperately come to the end of ourselves and are about to lose all hope, that we find our answers...that we confront our destroyer."

"I know you are right," Padah whispered.

"Despite your love for the shepherd, the pain of your past hindered you from entering into new depths of trust with him. You have yet to discover the extent of the kind shepherd's love for you. In that revelation you will truly begin to understand his ways. There you'll find the key to overcoming the fears that have held you captive, allowing you to reclaim your peace. You must continue to hold on to your faith in him, Padah. He will come for you, and he will not be late."

"But if I go to the east, he is not there;
if I go to the west, I do not find him.
When he is at work in the north, I do not see him;
when he turns to the south, I catch no glimpse of him.
But he knows the way that I take; when he has tested me,
I will come forth as gold. My feet have closely followed his steps;
I have kept his ways without turning aside." –Job 23:8-11 NIV

CHAPTER FOURTEEN

SHADOWLANDS

Encouraged by Joy's visit, Padah was determined to stand strong. The truth and wisdom of Joy's words still resonated within her mind as Mara walked up.

"Was that Joy I saw you and Eve talking to at the fence?"

"Yes! I have looked for her often but not found her. It isn't surprising, I guess. She rarely gets close to the old man's property. We had a wonderful conversation about the shepherd. I have missed her nearly as much as my twins," Padah said.

"I miss her too," Mara nodded in agreement. "She was the one member of the flock that I always felt accepted me as I was."

"Joy is like that. Walking with the kind shepherd has made her very wise. Her kindness and compassion are most rare. Placing trust in the shepherd rather than the sheep has spared her from many disappointments and given her a freedom to accept others as they are."

"Sheep will fail you every time!" Mara groaned. "Don't expect and you won't be disappointed! If only I could do that. How does she ever get past someone like Zula? And Huldah? I am so weary of their kind!"

"It hasn't been easy, even for Joy. She has paid a great price for the contentment and happiness she now enjoys. Her determined pursuit of the kind shepherd and her trust in him has set her free from many things. It has made her who she is! The time has come for us to do the same. We must leave all this behind, Mara, for we simply can't afford otherwise!"

"I know that's how I should feel, Padah. But as much as I loathe this place, I simply shudder at the thought of facing Zula and Ursula again! And now, looking as I do, they will most certainly torment me, and even worse, feel justified in doing so!"

"Only if you give them the power to do it, Mara. It was our fear of others and our lack of trust in the shepherd that got us here in the first place. This is not our home!"

"You're right, Padah! Now that I think of it, I have spent too much time in a place I really don't belong. Besides that," she paused in thought, "I refuse to give Zula or Ursula any further satisfaction!"

Padah nodded her head in agreement. "I am so glad to hear you say that! It makes this whole ugly experience count for something."

Smiling for the first time since their reunion, Mara added, "Eve, and even Huldah, have been touched by your words and encouraging example. You have given us hope when we had nearly given up."

"Even Huldah?" Padah teased. "Now, that is a miracle!"

Thankful for the comfort of their friendship, both Padah and Mara walked together toward a solitary tree in the old man's pasture in search of some shade. Feeling weak and very warm, Padah lay down on the cracked, dusty ground under its branches. Mara stood close by, her eyes scanning the sparse landscape for something to nibble.

"I need some rest right now. It seems I have not gotten enough lately," Padah sighed.

Padah soon drifted off, and several hours went by before she awoke. Hot and thirsty, she hadn't the strength to move. As time passed, her temperature continued to climb and her breathing became labored.

"Padah, you have slept nearly the entire day away! What is the matter?" Mara inquired. "I have been watching you all afternoon."

"I am not sure. But I am too weak to get up and burning with fever. I can hardly catch my breath. What do you suppose it is?" she asked Mara.

"I do not know. Just try to rest as much as you can until the old man takes us in for the night."

Sensing something unusual, Eve began to make her way over to Padah. On her heels came a curious Huldah, who could no longer restrain herself.

"Are we having somewhat of a problem here?" Huldah chortled.

"Nothing we can't handle," Mara returned, her voice cold.

"I'd say you're not handling it very well, since Padah's still on the ground and appears unable to get up!"

"I'm just not feeling well," Padah answered.

"Are you hurting?" Eve inquired.

"Not really. I have a fever and it's difficult to breathe."

"Obvious case of pneumonia, if you ask me!" Huldah spouted.

"No one did!" retorted Mara.

Ignoring her rebuke, Huldah continued, "You won't survive it, you know! Probably responsible for more sheep deaths than anything else. And there's no cure."

"And if you don't leave us alone now, it will be the death of you!" Mara countered.

"Some sheep just can't handle the truth! That's always been a challenge for you, hasn't it, Mara?"

Content with getting in the last word, Huldah huffed away.

"I don't know which one is more despicable, Huldah or Zula!" Mara exclaimed.

"She is terribly unhappy. In her own strange way, I think she's just trying to fit in," Eve responded.

"Well, she won't fit in with me! How can you have mercy for her after the unforgivable thing she did to you?" asked Mara incredulously.

"I will admit at first I was devastated. I found the pain nearly unbearable. But I realized that if I continued to focus on my loss, I would never be free. If I did not forgive her, I would soon become a prisoner to my unhappiness. I chose to forgive and pity her for such a desperate act. It speaks so loudly of her own need."

"What you say may be true, Eve, but I just can't excuse her that easily."

"I understand how you feel. But right now we must do something to get the old man's attention! I am so worried about Padah."

The two sheep began to bleat wildly, but their cries for attention unfortunately went unheeded as once again the moon and the stars claimed their rightful place in the black evening sky.

Padah hardly noticed the coolness of the night. Her body temperature rose higher, leaving her weak and her tenacious spirit drained. Feeling helpless, Eve and Mara watched their once vibrant friend lay languishing in the dirt at their feet.

"I know he will come for her very soon," a voice said. " Just you wait and see."

Startled, the two sheep quickly turned their heads to find Hope standing behind them.

"How do you know?" they chimed as one.

"Because the kind shepherd is never late!"

"How do you know that about the kind shepherd, anyway?"

"I have seen him come repeatedly to rescue so many the old man has stolen and maimed," Hope announced with confidence.

"Did you belong to the kind shepherd too?" Eve asked.

"No. But I can tell you this: I live for the day that he comes for me as well. He is my only hope! I have watched him from a distance for many years. There is no one in this entire valley as kind as he."

"Hope," Padah whispered. "Interesting isn't it? In my darkest hour when I finally think that I may never see the kind shepherd again because I am too sick to make the journey, I find inspiration because of your name!"

"Yes, and that is my gift to you, Padah, that I might encourage you not to lose your desire! You have traveled so far in search of your way back home to the shepherd. You mustn't cease to have heart now, even though you are at your weakest, and this your most uncertain hour."

"But if I do have pneumonia, I'll never recover. I'll just hold the rest of you back in your travel to the highlands." Padah paused, her breath coming in short gasps. "It's quite possible that my journey may be over and yours beginning. After all, I have already had my time with the shepherd. As much as I want to go back home, I cannot think of jeopardizing your chance for a safe and happy future."

"You don't even know if you have pneumonia!" Mara interjected.

"What else could it possibly be? My lungs are filling and I do not even have enough strength to stand up!"

"I don't know, but I can't stand to believe that, and you mustn't either!" Mara insisted.

"Mara's right!" Eve added. "We won't leave you."

Although she had moved away, Huldah had eavesdropped on the three friends.

"We must use our heads!" she shouted. "Padah is most likely contagious and endangering all of us! This expedition to the highlands requires a strong, healthy flock. She would only hold the rest of us back!"

"And who invited you anyway? Just what we need, one more bossy old ewe!" Mara retorted.

"Well, someone's got to lead. It might as well be the most level-headed of the group!" Huldah commanded.

"Don't you think we ought to wait for the kind shepherd?" Eve suggested, intervening between Mara and Huldah.

"What we really need right now is rest," Hope said.

"It looks like we'll be up on our feet again tonight. I don't see any signs of the old man," Eve added disappointedly. "We must stand by Padah since she cannot rise to her feet."

A hush descended upon the flock, and each silently agreed to guard their friend.

A full moon rose high into the night, while apprehension and uncertainty weighed on each sheep. Once again, the barking of dogs and yip of coyotes threatened their sleep.

Silent and spent, Padah lay motionless in the dust for several hours, able only to think upon the shepherd she so loved and longed for. She thought to herself, if he never comes back for me, I will continue to love him. Though I may not understand, I will trust him.

With eyes closed, she did not notice the imposing shadow that suddenly covered her own. It was the familiar touch upon her head and the softness of his voice that caused her heart to nearly leap from her chest.

"Padah."

It is him, she thought to herself.

"Padah."

He is here! My shepherd has finally come! Overcome with excitement, Padah struggled to greet him, but could not get to her feet. Instead, she collapsed into his arms. Noticing that the shepherd's arrival went unnoticed by the other sheep who continued to sleep, Padah looked into his face, confused.

"Do not worry about the others right now. They are not yet ready. I heard your heart cry out for me with such deep longing. Your hour of release has come."

Kneeling down beside her, his strong embrace and loving arms enveloped her as his salty tears dropped onto her dirty, white wool.

"Are you ready to come back to the highlands, Padah? I have missed you so very much!"

Weeping openly, his head rested atop her own, his tanned weathered hands clinging to her small frame as if refusing to let go. The shepherd cradled Padah throughout the night, his love filling her heart to overflowing. Waking nearly every hour, she rejoiced in his presence. Padah had never known such intense happiness was possible.

It was worth everything she had gone through. Her kind shepherd had come for her at last! And with his arrival, all slept safely the remainder of the night.

"Ah, I hear him—my lover!
Here he comes,
leaping on the mountains
and bounding over the hills.
My lover is like a swift gazelle or a young deer.
Look, there he is behind the wall!
Now he is looking in through the window,
gazing into the room.
My lover said to me,
'Rise up, my beloved, my fair one, and come away.
For the winter is past,
and the rain is over and gone.
The flowers are springing up,
and the time of singing birds has come,
even the cooing of turtledoves.
The fig trees are budding,
and the grapevines are in blossom.
How delicious they smell! Yes, spring is here!
Arise my beloved, my fair one and come away.'"
–Song of Songs 2:8-13 NLT

*S*ONG
OF THE
TURTLEDOVE

When the bright, orange sky announced the arrival of early morning, Padah first noticed the song of the turtledove overhead. Its mournful and tender summons could not be denied.

"Beautiful, isn't he?" the kind shepherd said as Padah peered up at the small, slender bird.

"The turtledove is seldom seen, because it lives in the deep forests and the high clefts of the rock. But the male's sad cooing for his mate in spring is unmistakable. Unlike most other kinds of birds, the dove mates for life and grieves in the absence of his love. His eyes are not made to look to either side, but are only capable of looking straight ahead. He has eyes for only one."

As she turned her head to search the deep blue pools of the shepherd's eyes, Padah's heart nearly stopped, for his all-consuming presence and deep love soothed her weary soul, its power beyond what she could imagine.

"When I lost you, Padah, and could find you nowhere, my own heart grew heavy within me and mourned like a dove."

Mourned like a dove. The same emptiness she felt deep inside her own heart, the kind shepherd had felt for her.

Desiring nothing other than to bask in the light and warmth of his love, Padah closed her eyes once again. Picturing herself resting along the edge of an endless ocean, she began to relax, allowing fresh waves of tranquility to roll over her.

Aware of Padah's thoughts, the kind shepherd spoke softly, "Yes, my 'redeemed one,' rest in my presence and allow every fear, anxiety, and sorrow to be cast into the deep sea of my love. Allow the healing power of my presence to wash over you, refreshing and restoring your body, soul, and spirit. Let nothing else be of concern to you."

Carried by the gentle currents of his love, Padah soon found herself swept into the depths of an incredibly sweet communion. The kind shepherd's voice beckoned her still further until it became as the deep rich sound of many rushing waters. His words were soon swallowed up in a bountiful outpouring of joy and peace too wonderful for words to express. So life-giving was this union of spirit and soul, Padah knew she would not only be healed, but continue to serve him with every remaining breath she had to give. Truly she belonged to him. She was no longer her own, for she now shared one heart with her kind shepherd.

"My dove in the clefts of the rock,
in the hiding places on the mountainside,
show me your face, let me hear your voice;
for your voice is sweet, and your face lovely.
My lover is mine and I am his..."
–Song of Songs 2:14,16 NIV

JOURNEY HOME

Padah rested well, reclaiming both her strength and vitality. Her friends, however, saw only that her limp body lay motionless on the ground. Convinced she would never have the chance to see her kind shepherd again, they felt her fate certain, wondering what would become of themselves as well.

When Padah finally opened her eyes, the kind shepherd was not in sight. He had left in search of the old man. Instead, she found both Eve and Mara looking down upon her frame with anxious eyes. Had his visit simply been a dream? Deciding not to add to her friends' confusion, Padah kept both her thoughts and her questions to herself. Not only would they find her experience difficult to believe, but it was far too precious to share.

"Padah, we had nearly given you up for dead!" Mara said, mystified.

"You have been down on the ground for nearly two days!" Eve added, eyes wide.

Padah smiled at her friends. "But I am so much better now. My fever is gone and I can actually breathe just like I did before my illness. I even feel like eating again!"

"That's wonderful news! It is so good to have you back with us again. We just couldn't leave you behind when we traveled to the highlands with the shepherd!" Hope exclaimed.

Struggling to get up on her feet, Padah felt woozy at first, then regained her composure.

It felt so good to be back on her feet again, so exciting to be standing alongside her friends. With each passing moment, she rejoiced in her second chance for life. Whether what she had experienced with the shepherd was real or a dream, Padah realized her life had begun anew. She was going home where she belonged.

Startled suddenly by movement just beyond the gate, all turned their heads in unison.

"Look!" Mara whispered. "It's him! The kind shepherd has come!"

While Eve, Mara, and Hope began to move toward him, Padah could only stand awestruck, taking in the magnificence of his presence, her heart swelling with both joy and gratitude. Now she knew he had come the night before. It had not been a dream after all. Somehow, things would never be the same again. A change had taken place within her. Why it had all transpired, she did not know, but remained something she had yet to discover.

"Come, Padah, and see what I have prepared for you," the shepherd invited.

Strangely, the other sheep did not seem to hear when he spoke to her alone. Yet, when he spoke to all of them at once, they heard and understood.

Yes, I have so much more to learn about my shepherd, Padah thought to herself.

The kind shepherd continued calling the sheep to himself when Huldah, forgotten by the others, quickly bounded up to the fence.

"Don't tell me she will be coming with us on our trip home!" Mara screeched in dismay.

"She does bear the kind shepherd's earmark and therefore does not belong here any more than we do," Eve conceded.

"Hope deserves to go before Huldah," Mara insisted.

"But Hope does not bear the mark of the kind shepherd. The old man still owns her," Eve pointed out.

"Not any more!" Huldah declared. "I heard the old man talking to the shepherd a little while ago. He took money from the kind shepherd's hands and then spit on him. The old man continued yelling at the kind shepherd as he walked away. I think he paid for Hope too! He would have taken more sheep but the old man had them locked up!"

"Is there anything you don't know?" Mara growled.

"Nope!" Huldah countered proudly.

Determined to establish her leadership, Huldah pushed her way to the front of the group. With head held high, she led the others as they followed on the heels of the shepherd. Passing single file through the old man's rickety gate, the five sheep and their devoted shepherd did not look back.

Thinking the return trip to the kind shepherd's property would be a short one, Padah was surprised when he unexpectedly turned south rather than north, leading them in exactly the opposite direction of the highlands where he lived.

This does not make any sense at all, she thought to herself. Why would he take us on such a long journey home when it was less than a day's trip if he followed the most direct path? Padah could only trust and follow his perplexing lead. If there were only one thing that she had learned from her terrible ordeal, it was that only by following the shepherd would she be assured of her life.

The brilliant penetrating sun rose until it sat directly overhead. So excited had the flock been that the long hours of travel seemed like minutes. But though their hearts were light, their minds remained heavy in thought. Too much had happened to dismiss the past so easily. Only time spent with the kind shepherd, and their physical as well as emotional separation from their tormenting past, could eventually free their spirits and heal their hearts.

Approaching a small, rippling brook, the kind shepherd knelt down to fill a large cistern of water. He then carefully poured the water into a hand-made well he had hastily made. After several trips to fill the well, the kind shepherd saw that the tired flock had quenched their thirst. The sheep lay to rest under a huge shade tree. Deeply content, the small flock dozed and rejuvenated their weary souls as the hours of the long afternoon passed in the presence of their kind shepherd.

"You have made
known
to me
the path of life;
you fill me with joy
in your presence,
with eternal pleasures at your
right hand."
–Psalm 16:11 NIV

CHAPTER SEVENTEEN

NARROW PASSAGE

When the late afternoon sun sank lower into the deep blue horizon and the sheep had sufficiently rested, the kind shepherd encouraged them to rise once again to their feet. There were yet several hours before nightfall in which the kind shepherd could find a much more suitable resting place for his small flock.

The five sheep obediently followed behind the shepherd as he led them up gentle slopes, taking pleasure in their new surroundings. The rocky, barren, parched lands of the Valley of Achor had given way to low-growing green shrubbery. The foothills in the near distance welcomed them, and the looming mountains behind beckoned as well. The majestic peaks, draped softly in their bluish-purple hues, sat in stark contrast to the lifeless brown dust that the sheep had become so accustomed to. Only Huldah displayed signs of discontentment as she mumbled and sighed under her breath.

"I really don't know what could be in the shepherd's mind leading us along these old rutted paths. Now we have so much farther to travel! If I had my way we would be cutting across the meadows, heading directly to where the shepherd's highlands begin. It's an easier journey by far. But, then, I'm only a sheep and not the shepherd."

"Thank goodness for that!" Mara chimed in muffled agreement.

Padah could not help but notice the new perspective and panoramic view that came with each step up the hill. The surrounding land was something she never had the opportunity to see. She could only wonder how much of what she was looking at actually belonged to the kind shepherd. The Valley of Achor below narrowed as the sheep ascended in their climb, until it appeared only as a black and menacing scar against the green backdrop. Strange, she thought to herself, how insignificant it seems in comparison to the kind shepherd's highlands.

The small flock of sheep continued in their slow, steady climb up the slopes until they reached a lovely meadow that spread out invitingly before them. Just like a blanket unfolding in preparation for a wonderful picnic, the lush sweet grasses were no doubt chosen by their kind shepherd and intended to satisfy their hunger, providing a most delectable treat.

He always surprises me, Padah thought to herself.

Close to the meadow's edge, Padah spotted a beautiful lake so clear that she could nearly see to the bottom. Its transparent blue depths stood cool and undisturbed as glass, reflecting only the tall dark forest along its far edge.

"We will spend the night here," the shepherd declared.

Because his flock was out in the open, he searched the surrounding area for some type of protection. Finding an assortment of large rocks that had been placed in a formation with three sides, very much like a sheepfold, he smiled with satisfaction.

"This will work very nicely," he reassured his flock. "You will be safe until morning. We must start very early tomorrow if we are to clear the narrow passage before dark."

The sun had now spent itself on another day, leaving only a glorious crimson trail in the sky. The bright red-orange glow and the subsequent hot-pink streaks were but a promise of the sun's return.

Was there anything more glorious than being reunited with her shepherd and watching him enjoy the splendor of a spectacular sunset? Padah thought not. With that final thought she allowed herself to drift peacefully to sleep.

Although the purple darkness of night was only too eager to overtake the sky, it too had its rewards. The bright carpet of twinkling stars that followed the sunset kept the lonely shepherd company throughout the long night as he faithfully guarded the only thing that mattered to him…his sheep.

When morning arrived, the well-rested flock were eager to accompany their shepherd in his pilgrimage up the hills. After savoring the lush grasses and drinking from the lake, they resumed their journey to the highlands. The sparrows and starlings chirped their joyful commands along the way as the sheep climbed single-file up the sides of the steep hills behind their guide.

By midmorning, the distance between the hills shortened considerably, creating deep ravines and sharp canyons. Without realizing the extent of their incline, the sheep had reached tremendous heights, the winds whipping and whistling their way through the narrow divides.

"We will be entering the narrow passage very soon," said the kind shepherd. "You must stay very close behind me now. Follow every step I take and do not stray. There will be room for only one at a time to pass through. I will guide and instruct each one of you individually. Although you will feel alone I will not leave you, but apart from absolute obedience to my directions, you will not cross safely. "

The sheep followed the shepherd as the path wound around the side of the hill, where they were greeted by a formidable sight: the narrow passage flanked by frighteningly steep cliffs, just as the shepherd had described it. The rocks below looked like sharp-edged scissors prepared to cut into pieces whoever dared slip from the narrow path above. Eve was the first sheep to approach the passage.

"I cannot possibly make it through!" she cried. "Isn't there any other way we can go? She looked down at her quivering legs. "I am shaking so, I will most certainly lose my balance and fall!"

"Padah, you go first," suggested Mara. "That will encourage her."

"But I am not a good one to follow. My bad leg is so unsteady, it could easily collapse beneath me," Padah responded. "You know fear has always been a weakness of mine. Please go first."

"You are the one who most clearly understands the shepherd's voice. It would be so much easier for us if we could follow your lead. Please be brave and go first!" Mara pleaded.

"You are all arguing unnecessarily, quibbling like a group of silly cowards!" snapped Huldah. "Haven't you noticed that if we merely back up a bit we can step over to the opposite side of the canyon where the bank is much broader and avoid all of this? Why there's even room for several of us at one time to pass through without danger." She surveyed the others, her eyes sharp. "So, who is going to follow me?"

Confused, Mara glanced in the direction of the shepherd when he began to coax her to begin the procession.

"Yes, Mara, go ahead. You can make it, I know you can," he gently encouraged.

Angling her neck to look at Huldah, Mara stood frozen.

Once again Huldah argued, "You will regret it! He won't be able to help you once you've fallen to your death!"

The shepherd patiently beckoned Mara a second time, but she began to back up, her thin legs trembling from fear. "It's okay Mara," he sympathized, "you can follow the others."

"Please, Padah, come join me for the sake of the other sheep," he urged.

Surprised and anxious, Padah looked into the shepherd's kind eyes.

"I need you to be strong. You must lead," he insisted, extending his arm toward her.

The midday wind had picked up, blowing with all its might, pushing at the backs of Padah's already quivering knees. As she looked down at her feet, she felt dizzy and light-headed.

"Do not look down, Padah! Slowly, take one step at a time. Keep your eyes on me," the kind shepherd directed.

As Padah took her first step, some pebbles slid out from under her feet. Hearing them crack as they fell to the depths in the canyon below nearly caused her to lose balance. The whistling howl of the wind, the spillage of rocks under her feet, all horrified her beyond what she thought herself capable of enduring.

"I am here, Padah, and you can make it. Think only of what you must do. Keep looking at me. Trust me, Padah, I will not let you fall."

Focusing all her concentration on the shepherd, Padah continued to traverse the narrow passage in front of her. With each step the shepherd gently prodded. Not once did she look at the terrifying abyss below her. Thinking she would never reach the end of the passage, Padah pressed on, barely breathing. Engrossed as she was in her mission, she did not even see the two hands that stretched out to receive her quaking body.

"You made it!" he cheered, beaming with joy. "I knew I could depend on you to follow me!"

The four other sheep stood watching in fear, their apprehension growing more intense knowing their turn approached.

Realizing that being last meant being even more alone, Eve stepped forward next. Inspired by Padah's triumphant crossing, Eve pushed her fears aside and looked ahead to the shepherd.

"Come on, Eve, you can do this too!" the shepherd prompted.

Obediently, Eve followed the narrow path while keeping her eyes on the shepherd's face. Although equally terrified, she kept thinking of the rewards that awaited her on the highlands.

Hope was the next to successfully cross the treacherous chasm. Her desire to belong to the shepherd compelled her every step. The strong winds and falling rocks under foot did not deter her from her mission nor steal her sweet victory.

When Mara's turn finally arrived, Huldah's efforts to encourage her to cross to the opposite side of the canyon had nearly succeeded. They were as strong a pull as the winds that tugged at her body.

"We can go together," Huldah urged. "There is more than one way to do anything, I tell you. Why subject yourself to needless danger when there's an easier way?"

The lonely howl of the wind picked up the sound of distant shouts, startling both Mara and Huldah. Strangers were approaching. They were not willing to allow the kind shepherd and his flock to travel in peace, for the old man's hate for the shepherd had fueled his desire to torment them.

"The old man is coming for the shepherd and his sheep!" Huldah shouted. "I can smell that man from miles away. If we do not go now we will be caught for sure. I'm leaving and if you're smart you will do the same. There is not time to take the narrow passage even if we wanted to!"

Breaching the small separation, Huldah found space to stand on the opposite side of the canyon. Watching her from the other side, Mara felt confused, unable to decide which way she should go and whose direction she should follow.

Huldah did not wait for Mara to join her, but charged ahead in fear as the sound of voices drew near.

"Huldah, come back!" the kind shepherd called. "Do not go that way!"

But it was too late for Huldah. The winds carried away the shepherd's pleading call to his misguided sheep. Only Mara could catch his voice. Driven by panic, Huldah climbed recklessly, stumbling as the dirt and rocks beneath her feet broke away. Frantically, she clawed at the ledge trying to gain a foot-hold. But it would not bear her weight, and Huldah helplessly cascaded over the edge of the cliff onto the rocks below, where her broken body lay.

Utterly horrified and in shock, the unsuspecting sheep and their saddened shepherd spoke not a word. Mara stood paralyzed in disbelief.

"Don't look, Mara," the shepherd spoke firmly. "Don't be afraid."

But despite her desire to follow the others, Mara stood violently shaking, immobilized by her fear. Terrified after witnessing the death of Huldah, her stomach churned in anguish, and her head grew dizzy.

I simply cannot make it, she decided. I have no choice but to turn back.

Concerned for her safety, the kind shepherd moved toward her. Gently he reached over, cautiously bending down as he lifted her up into his arms. Drawing her close to his body, the kind shepherd held her tightly, whispering into her ear, "You, too, are safe, my precious one. Do you know how grateful I am to have you with me once again? Very soon, you will be home on the highlands." He placed her gently on the ground again next to the others.

Relieved by Mara's safe crossing, Padah marveled at the love and mercy the kind shepherd had for all his flock. There is not another like him anywhere, she concluded.

Once through the passage, the kind shepherd led the remaining four members of his small group to an open meadow where they could graze and drink from a mountain stream. A cave nearby offered welcome shelter for the night.

While the sheep rested, the heartbroken shepherd sat at the opening of the shelter. Padah watched the body of her shepherd as it shook silently. Knowing he was grieving over the loss of Huldah, Padah moved closer to the edge of his clothing. Snuggling against his side, she became keenly aware of the inconsolable sadness that gripped him. She could not help but feel his deep distress. If only she were able to comfort him as he had done for her so many times.

"I will instruct you and
teach you in the way you should go;
I will counsel you
and watch over you."
–Psalm 32:8 NIV

CHAPTER EIGHTEEN

OUNTAINS OF PRAISE

Not easily forgotten, the tragic death of Huldah impacted not only the shepherd but the rest of the flock. Mara had eaten little, her feelings of guilt and remorse hung as a chafing rope around her neck.

"Mara, you cannot blame yourself," the kind shepherd told her. "Huldah chose to go her own way. She found it difficult to trust anyone but herself. She hardened her heart against my instruction."

Mara could not forget the awful words she had spoken, the hate she had felt for Huldah. She had even wished her dead at times. Now that it had come to pass, she was sick at heart.

From their new vantage point, they could still see the narrow passage and the crumpled body of Huldah on the rocks below. Strangely, her body was not alone. A number of men lay still beside her.

Drawing his small flock close to himself, the kind shepherd began to speak.

"I want you to look at the sides of the narrow passage. Do you see something?" he asked.

Stretching their necks to look, the sheep peered in the direction of the passageway they wanted only to put behind them. But the shepherd, desiring to spare them future mistakes, insisted upon their attention.

"The sheer cliffs on the sides of the narrow passage are supported by deep layers of rock, but the opposite side of the ravine, where Huldah crossed, is held up only by sand and sediment. It is very unstable, capable of giving way at any moment. Huldah could not see the difference. Her only guide was my voice, which she refused to listen to." A deep sorrow crept into the shepherd's eyes. "She resented my leadership, thinking the shorter, easier path through the meadows to the highlands would be preferable. But the old man, leading the townspeople in their pursuit of me, would have overtaken us easily if we had gone that way. Though the meadows were closest, I chose instead to take you to the highlands by way of the narrow passage. Otherwise, we were openly vulnerable to the assault of our enemies. I am the only one who knew the way through the narrow passage. The bodies of the men you saw next to Huldah's met the same sad fate as she did in their search for us."

Unaware that they had been followed, Padah stood wondering why.

Responding to her unspoken thoughts, the shepherd continued. "The old man will not give up easily that which he has lost. He will use any means to reclaim what once was his. Through his deception of the townspeople, he will find unwitting help.

"And Huldah, do not judge her too harshly. The abuse and torment she suffered at the hands of the old man made it impossible for her to trust any man after that. My heart grieves deeply for her. I so wanted to heal her wounds, which she tried to cover with her callous indifference. Her weakness, unlike an outward limp noticeable to all, was a broken heart, which she chose to mask with false pride. Because others did not understand, she stood alone and misunderstood in her time of need."

The kind shepherd turned and began beckoning his flock to ascend the foothills leading to the Mountains of Praise. Despite their sorrow, the ewes followed, knowing the highlands sat beyond. Padah could hardly wait to see Joy, the twins, and all her friends once again.

But the climb was not easy. Left weary from the events of the day before, Padah found the new challenge exhausting.

My heart is just not in this journey today, she thought to herself.

Proving much more arduous than originally anticipated, the climb soon became a test of her endurance. Placing one foot in front of the next, she forced herself to push on, though she was often tempted to stop. The kind shepherd, however, did not cease in his efforts to urge her on.

The struggling sheep eventually scaled the first peak. Not only had the air become much lighter, but the sun shone brighter, for they had risen above the dark clouds below. The view by now was truly magnificent.

Stopping so that the sheep could graze and drink for a while, the kind shepherd proudly announced, "You have scaled victoriously the Mountains of Sorrow. The dark shadows of heaviness that weighed you down have now been left behind."

Greatly relieved, the four sheep drank deeply from the refreshing mountain runoff that trickled into a pool at the foot of nearby rocks. The tantalizing shrubs and sweet grasses at the base of the boulders delighted their palates and soothed their hungry souls. The warm, penetrating sun upon their backs felt good and was a welcome relief from the dreary, damp clouds of the valley and foothills before.

After the sheep's brief rest, they resumed their journey up to the Mountains of Praise.

The winds pushed against their faces and the broad, rocky paths beneath their feet narrowed. Once again, they heard the familiar voices of the townsmen behind them. Unprepared for the reappearance of their pursuers, the distressed sheep began to shake with fear.

"You will not get away with this! Liar! You cannot outrun us forever."

"Pay no attention to their threats," the kind shepherd instructed.

But the men, infuriated by their unheeded shouts, hurled stones at the sheep, chipping away at the sides of the mountain as they hit.

Terrified, Mara froze.

"Look at me, Mara!" the shepherd called. "Do not stop climbing. Follow me closely."

A large rock whistled through the air, striking Mara's foot and causing her to stumble. As she lost her balance, the shepherd's long arm reached down, steadying her and guiding her back to the path.

"Come on, take another step, Mara," he persuaded.

Hesitating, she looked back, fearing her enemies were gaining. As she did so, a second, larger stone struck her head. Stunned by the impact, Mara fell helplessly backward. Within seconds, the kind shepherd dropped down onto the path next to her. Shielding Mara's body with his own, he took the brunt of their adversaries' attack.

"Hope, Eve, Padah! Climb as fast as you can past Mara up the path with eyes focused on the summit until you reach it," he instructed. "Let nothing distract you along the way! We are in the midst of a battle, but if you do as I say we are assured of the victory!"

The kind shepherd revived Mara with a drink from the cool, refreshing water he carried on him.

"Mara, I have given you the support and strength you need to overcome, but you must stay closer to me than ever. Press in to my side as you take your steps and I will carry the weight of your body against my own. We will make it only if you do not look back again in fear. You cannot give up!"

Slowly, steadily, the shepherd and Mara made their way to the top of the path where Eve, Padah, and Hope waited patiently. Exhausted, Mara collapsed to her knees. The kind shepherd knelt over her, the blood from his wounds seeping through the torn clothing on his back, wounds made by the hurled stones from which he had shielded Mara.

"You have done a very courageous thing, Mara. You did not stray from the path of praise in spite of the vicious attacks of your enemies, in spite of your great fear. You have truly triumphed!" He turned to the rest of his flock. "None of you will see their faces again on our journey home. In conquering the summit of fear, you have finally left your enemies behind. They are incapable of following you past the high places of praise!"

After a time of rest and refreshment, the kind shepherd took his small flock over the majestic summits of Peace and Joy. The tranquility they experienced now far surpassed anything they had ever known.

"*For our struggle is not against*
flesh and blood,
but against the rulers,
against the authorities,
against the powers of this dark world
and against the spiritual forces
of evil in the heavenly realms."
–Ephesians 6:12 NIV

CHAPTER NINETEEN

DESERT ROSE

Not wanting to leave their tranquil setting, the sheep desired only to linger, but the kind shepherd gently encouraged them to press onward in their journey home. Slowly they began to descend the craggy backside of the mountains that overlooked the deserted wasteland below, a stark contrast to their exhilarating mountain-top experience. Padah could only trust in the shepherd's wisdom as she ventured down the steep cliffs behind him.

"Never have I seen such a desolate wilderness!" commented Eve.

"Even our enemies would not dare follow us to such a forsaken place!" Mara agreed.

"However shall we find food and water where hardly a shade tree can be found? Perhaps this is not our destination," Eve suggested.

"I'm sure it isn't. Certainly the good shepherd would not have brought us here to stay for long," Hope agreed.

"He doesn't think the way we do," Padah reassured them. "He knows where he is taking us. Had we not followed his instruction earlier and cut through the meadows as Huldah suggested, we would have ended up in the hands of the angry townsmen and the old man. The kind shepherd has kept us safe, despite their ugly threats. Here, too, surely he must have a plan."

No sooner had the sun dipped behind the far mountains on the opposite side of the wasteland than the shepherd and his humble flock reached the desert floor. The sand, still hot from the searing rays of the afternoon sun, provided welcome warmth from the rapidly approaching chill of the night. Patiently the shepherd watered his thirsty flock from a jug he had filled earlier from a stream. Much to their surprise the sheep found a cozy camp near a broad, leafy bush. As the four sheep fed and settled down for the night, their sovereign leader sat perched atop a rock close by and began to play his flute. There he entertained himself long into the night, comforting not only his own weary soul, but those of his sheep. By his side sat his rod and staff. Frightening as the sound of the jackals were, Padah knew she no longer had anything to fear.

Morning had barely arrived when Padah and the rest of the sheep opened their eyes to witness a most unusual sight. Raking the sand surrounding them was the shepherd. Suddenly he spotted something. He took a bottle from his waist and poured what looked like oil in a circle. When he finished, he allowed his sheep to rise.

Noticing their eyes upon him, the shepherd remarked with a chuckle, "It's okay, I have vanquished your enemies for now!"

What enemies could he be referring to, Padah wondered, as she had seen nothing but circles in the sandy sediment.

"This field has an infestation of sand vipers," he explained. "They are hiding in the sand and would like nothing more than to catch you unexpectedly and bite you on the nose, poisoning you with their deadly venom. But with their smooth bodies, the vipers are incapable of passing over the oil. They are now captive to their surroundings," he smiled happily. "And I know only too well how much you will avoid the hole, since you do not relish the smell of the oil! Just the same, you must come close and allow me to apply my oil to your heads. In this way I can protect you from the sunstroke you would otherwise expose yourself to while in the desert."

After applying the oil, the kind shepherd poured forth water from his jug and even pulled some sweet grass out from under his clothing. Feeding each sheep by hand, he led them along until they reached some sparse vegetation.

After two long, hot , exhausting days in the desert, the flock had become disheartened. The desert, Padah thought to herself, was a most inhospitable place. This part of the journey cannot end too soon.

"I cannot go another day like this," Mara sighed.

"I don't like it either," Hope agreed, "but what choice is there? We are sheep that cannot make it without the shepherd and this is where he is leading us."

"Well, tell me, what could possibly be gained by going this way? There has got to be some sort of a shortcut somewhere!" Mara added.

"Now you're beginning to sound like Huldah!" Eve said.

"I suppose," Mara sighed, her eyes scanning the new horizon. "No sheep would choose to spend time in a desert. It's dangerous, and difficult, without much food or water or even trees for shade. Sheep are simply not meant for this kind of life! We require rich pasture. We need to be free from the worry of wild animals and snakes," she added shaking her head. "I really do think we missed the trail somewhere."

None of the sheep replied, but silently followed on what seemed like a never-ending pilgrimage. As with Mara, they wondered what could possibly be gained from the experience. Was there a lesson to learn, some advantage to gain? Or was it, as Mara suggested, that they had simply wandered off course?

In their tired and disgruntled condition, the sheep didn't notice that the shepherd had led them to a small but lovely oasis. Out in the midst of their desolate surroundings sprang a grove of large palm trees and clusters of vegetation alongside an inviting brook. With its headwaters originating from the mountains nearby, the brook coursed through the oasis, sparkling like diamonds in the afternoon sun.

Playfully it meandered through the palms, splashing over the rocks lavishly as it zigzagged back and forth between both sun and shade.

Leaving the sheep just long enough to locate a place to rest his flock, the kind shepherd wandered a number of yards a way. When he returned, the sheep had already begun to delight in their unexpected refreshment in the desert.

As the shepherd settled down under a nearby palm tree, Padah looked up, keenly aware of the gentle breeze swaying the large leaves overhead.

Strange, she thought to herself, that something so enticingly beautiful and so restful can be found in the middle of a place so dreadfully barren and vexing to the soul.

"Padah, come here and rest with me," the kind shepherd invited. He said nothing for a long while as she relaxed at his side. An eagle appeared overhead, soaring effortlessly. Padah admired the wings spread wide, the graceful gliding, the simple majesty of the bird.

"The great thermals from the heat of the desert rise, enabling the eagle to soar with ease," the shepherd explained. "The eagle above all other animals exemplifies gratefulness, triumphing in the face of adversity by accepting difficulties as part of its great provision. As a symbol of strength and freedom, it soars to unbelievable heights from its rocky crag above its desolate domain. As a storm approaches, the eagle sees opportunity rather than opposition, for with that storm come intense thermal updrafts on which the eagle can fly much higher and farther.

"Padah, it is here in the midst of the wilderness that you must learn to rest. As the oasis is found in the most unlikely places of the desert, so shall it be for you as you learn to trust and follow me wherever I lead you. Your adversity shall produce for you blessings and your provision shall not be lacking. Do not run any longer in the midst of the storm, but allow it to carry you to even greater heights. If you will dare to draw close to me in the wilderness, trusting and resting in my love for you, I will care for you as a mother eagle covers her young beneath her safe, strong wings."

The kind shepherd got up and walked over to a large bush with lovely purple flowers. Padah watched as he cut long stalks and carried them back to his resting place underneath the palm tree. Next, he spent a considerable amount of time carefully weaving the branches into a lovely wreath. Upon finishing, the kind shepherd unexpectedly reached over to Padah, gently placing the fragrant wreath over her head, allowing it to fall down around her neck.

"It is the Rose of Sharon," he said, "and you, one after my own heart, are my little rose in the desert."

And with that the kind shepherd began to sing to Padah a song unlike anything she had ever heard him sing before, a song from his own heart that penetrated into the very depths of her own.

"And the rose it shall bloom in the desert. Its beauty for all to behold. And its fragrance shall reach to the heavens...To the one who planted the rose."

"He gives power to those who are tired
and worn out; he offers strength to the weak.
But those who wait on the Lord
will find new strength.
They will fly high on wings like eagles.
They will run and not grow weary,
they will walk and not faint."
–Isaiah 40:29,31 NLT

"I have loved you, my people,
with an everlasting love.
With unfailing love I have drawn you to myself."
–Jeremiah 31:3 NLT

HEALING STREAMS

Following their leisurely rest at the oasis, the shepherd and his small flock moved on in their journey home. Marking a path through the wilderness, they could not help but notice overhead the large white thunderheads that continued to build higher and higher against the deep blue sky.

"We will need to find shelter for the night," the shepherd announced. "There is an unseasonable summer storm brewing."

Continuing to press on before sunset, the shepherd spotted a group of large rocks surrounding an opening in the side of the mountain.

"Here we are," he said, satisfied with his discovery. "This cave will do nicely."

Without water in sight, the shepherd poured from his jug into a hollowed-out rock for his sheep to drink. Using his rod to dislodge clumps of grass and leaves from the sparse vegetation that surrounded them, the shepherd fed them. The darkness fell rapidly, but the sheep rested contentedly within the shelter he had provided for them for the night.

The distant rumblings of thunder warned of the impending storm. With the wind beginning to gust through the lonely canyons of the desert, the sands whipped across the sheep's faces, stinging their eyes and noses. Moving backward into the rock formation, the sheep lowered their heads to their chests to shut out the nasty onslaught of gritty sand. As the loud winds roared, they drowned out even the eerie barking of jackals nearby. The once peaceful, bright day had suddenly turned into a night of foreboding blackness and intense threatening winds.

The kind shepherd sat in front of his sheep with only his rod, staff, and sling to protect himself. Even his usual small lantern was of no use tonight against the raging winds. Watching his silhouette as he sat crouched on the lonely ground with his long wool coat whipping fiercely back and forth, Padah realized how much her fondness for her shepherd had grown. The companionship of the other sheep no longer satisfied her as they once did. It was the closeness of the kind shepherd she now craved. He alone understood and cared for her every need, and in his bravery took upon himself the stones intended for Mara, sparing her life as well. He was the kindest and gentlest person she had ever known.

Padah left her three sleeping friends to inch her way up behind him. The kind shepherd unexpectedly opened wide his coat, inviting her to slip in under his arm next to his side.

"I have been waiting for you to seek me out," he said.

Shepherd and sheep sat quietly, watching the night storm pass, the warmth they shared and the oneness of their hearts sufficient to face any prevailing storm. The fierce thunder and lightning rumbled and crashed even more vigorously than the night of that fateful storm on the highlands. The torrents of rain flooded the desert ground, creating streams where there had been none before. But the shepherd, having taken his flock to higher ground, was not at all concerned.

When morning arrived, the stillness of the desert was interrupted only by the soft cooing of a turtledove. With the storm behind them, the morning seemed fresh with promise. Padah sensed that their wilderness journey was about to end.

"Do you see the hills, my little flock?" the shepherd asked. "We are drawing close to the foot of the highlands."

"Finally!" Mara breathed a sigh of relief. "I can hardly believe we made it this far!"

"But first we must cross through the healing streams just ahead." Water! No, not more water, Padah thought to herself.

Sheep feared water naturally, but after Padah's near-death experience with the flood, the mere thought of it absolutely terrified her. A sick feeling came upon her that she was unable to shake.

I will do nearly anything the kind shepherd asks of me, she thought to herself, but to wade through streams of water…that I cannot do!

With the desert mountains fading behind them, the shepherd led his group into the coolness of the forest's edge. The sound of rushing water announced the nearness of the stream. Padah's fear continued to mount, her body trembling uncontrollably as they drew closer.

At the stream's edge, the shepherd signaled his flock to stop.

"These are the streams that heal your body and soul. Until you pass through them, you will not be prepared to carry out my plans for you. It is here that you leave behind anything that will hinder you from moving into your new life. You will be cleansed of all you accumulated while on the old man's property. You can take none of it with you into the highlands. But before we cross over, you must first be rid of your dirty wool. I know how much you dislike the process, but you have become heavily matted and covered with mud, manure, burrs, and other debris. It will only weigh you down and create the possibility of your being cast down."

One by one the kind shepherd sheared his sheep. One by one their dirty coats fell away, leaving them naked and pure.

"Padah, you are going to lead the others as we pass through the healing streams. You must put your fear behind you. In your faithfulness to do so, you will find a wonderful surprise upon reaching the other side."

Despite the kind shepherd's reassurance, Padah remained panic-stricken at the edge of the bank, but her sickened heart feared even more his disappointment. How many times must I fail him from fear? she asked herself.

Reaching down for his rod and staff, the shepherd extended it toward Padah. Gently tucking it under her backside, he coaxed her lovingly into the cold water.

"I am here," he said, his strong voice melting her resolve and drawing her near.

With the shepherd's hand upon her back and gentle words to guide her, Padah waded through the clear waters. Eve, Mara, and Hope followed close behind.

Upon reaching the other side, the shepherd helped guide her onto the grassy bank along with the others.

"Look, Padah!" Hope exclaimed. "Look at your leg!"

As Padah glanced down, she noticed her once crooked and unsightly leg appeared to be straight.

"Walk on it, Padah. See if you still limp!" Eve urged.

Padah strolled over to where Mara stood and then back to Eve again.

Looking up into the shepherd's face in amazement, Padah waited for him to explain.

"It is true, Padah, you have been healed of your limp. When you followed me through the healing waters despite your great fright, fear lost its power over you once and for all. The leg that carried you obediently through the water, despite its lack of sure-footedness, was healed as well."

The sheep were so excited and astonished as a result of Padah's healing, they could speak of little else among themselves. They all shared in Padah's victory, for they knew how much she had suffered from her lameness.

But the shepherd was not through with his preparations. Calling Hope to his side, the shepherd removed the familiar knife that he had so often used.

"Today, Hope, you become part of my own flock," he said lovingly. "Never shall there be a question as to whom you belong. Never will the old man be able to claim you or take you from me again!"

As the shepherd painfully notched out her ear, marking her as his own, his eyes filled with tears. He had waited for a long time to answer the call of her heart. Now they would never be apart!

Again, the shepherd's sheep rejoiced over his great display of mercy.

"Mara, come near to me," the shepherd instructed. "You have always considered yourself the least and most undesirable among my sheep, but I tell you in my eyes you have become one of my most treasured. I have heard you cry out in darkness and I have understood your deep pain. From this day on, you shall no longer fear your enemies, for when they strike out at you, they in fact strike out at me. Instead of being the last, you shall be the first. As you continue to humble yourself and forgive, I will continue to lift you up and grant great mercy. You belong to me, Mara, and have found favor in my sight, for I have seen your heart." He then moved his hand slowly across her chest until it settled over her heart to heal it. "Today your name shall no longer be called Mara, which means 'bitter waters,' but Naomi, which means 'sweet and pleasant.'

"Eve, you, my little one, shall be the mother of many! Believe it or not, there will actually come a day when you will say to me, 'Need you bless me so much?' For in your fruitfulness of womb, I will need to multiply even more your patience!" The kind shepherd chuckled. "I have granted you the desire of your heart, Eve, and your offspring shall indeed be a blessing to us all!"

Pulling out his flask of olive oil, the shepherd once again poured oil over their heads. He then applied an ointment to their eyes to repel ticks, flies, and various other parasites.

"I am not a shepherd without my sheep, and you are helpless without your shepherd. But today I have given you all the power to have victory over your enemies as you walk closely by my side and continue to reside in my presence," he concluded.

And with that, the kind shepherd, along with his most humble flock, made their way up the grassy slopes to the familiar highlands, following their triumphant journey.

"And a highway will be there;
it will be called
the Way of Holiness.
The unclean will not journey on it.
No lion will be there,
nor will any ferocious beast get upon it;
they will not be found there.
But only the redeemed will walk there,
and the ransomed of the Lord will return.
They will enter Zion with singing;
everlasting joy will be upon their heads.
Gladness and joy will overtake them,
and sorrow and sighing will flee away."
–Isaiah 35:8-10 NIV

CHAPTER TWENTY-ONE

THE IGHLANDS

The joy and expectancy that filled Padah's heart as she made her way up to the highlands now energized her every step. Slowly ascending the dark green hillside, the small flock, with their jubilant shepherd, made the final wide turn leading onto the slopes of the meadows just before nightfall. Familiar as she was with the surroundings, the initial glimpse of the highlands against the Mountains of El Shaddai created a surge of excitement in her so strong that her heart began to race wildly.

I had nearly forgotten how incredibly beautiful the highlands of Menuca actually are, she thought to herself. So majestic, so tranquil, so utterly magnificent! At last I am home in the very place I thought I might never see again.

As she slowly scanned the horizon for signs of the shepherd's flock, Padah's eyes searched eagerly, hoping to spot both the twins and Joy somewhere amidst the meadows. The flock would no doubt have many questions about her abrupt departure and lengthy absence. They might misunderstand or even reject her. But Padah pressed on, for her exhilaration and desire to be united with those she loved far outweighed any other concerns she might have. She was no longer the same fearful sheep she had been when she had run away. So much had happened in only a few short weeks, but it was enough to transform her heart and mind forever. She could hardly wait to share the events with Joy!

"Oh! Oh my!" Hope gasped.

Fearing something was wrong, Mara, now Naomi, and Padah turned quickly to look back over their shoulders.

"Hope? Are you all right?" Padah inquired.

"How could you ever do it?" Hope asked.

"How could I ever do what?"

"How could you ever leave all this behind?"

Padah smiled. "I have asked myself the same question too many times. Isn't it the most heavenly place you have ever seen? And you haven't even been to the meeting place or journeyed with the shepherd up the slopes of the Mountains of El Shaddai, the mountains of the Almighty God," Padah added. "Just wait, Hope! There is so much for you to discover. Even if you lived here a lifetime, you could never experience it all!"

"Look!" Naomi said. "Part of the flock is lying underneath the tree."

Peacefully ruminating beside the stream, Zula rested along with several other sheep. Nakeh, Zak, and Joy were not among them. Spotting first the kind shepherd followed by his small flock, the sheep out in the meadow became curious about the approaching visitors and rose to their feet. Instead of bringing back just one, the shepherd led a group of four, and all eyes and ears were focused intently upon their arrival.

Without warning, the sound of approaching hooves drew closer.

"What...?" Startled, Naomi turned just in time to avoid a near collision.

Skidding to a newly practiced stop, Zak beamed proudly. Elated by his discovery, he shrieked with joy.

"You are alive! Grace said the kind shepherd would bring you back, that you wouldn't have left us forever!"

Looking up gratefully at the shepherd, Zak pressed tightly against Padah, seeking out her scent, wondering about the other sheep that stood by her. Padah closed her eyes, relishing the moment she once thought might never be.

Zak told her, "Nakeh is with Grace at the stream. They will be so surprised! I will go for them! Yahoo!" he cheered. With an effortless leap through the air, he burst into a lively gallop toward the stream, shouting the good news to all he passed.

"Well, if the rich meadows can do that for him, I should have returned a long time ago!" Naomi teased, still shaking from her unexpected encounter.

Stifling a giggle, Padah explained, "You can be gone for weeks, have your entire world turned upside down, and return home to find certain things have not changed at all! Naomi, that was my first-born, Zak!"

Catching the end of Padah's introduction, Melody sauntered up. In agreement she added, "The one thing we have not lacked for in your absence, Padah, is entertainment, thanks to Zak!"

"Melody, how wonderful to see you again! This is Naomi. Her name was Mara when she once lived here. Upon her return, however, the kind shepherd has given her a new name."

"You have picked up others along the way?" Melody inquired.

"Indeed we have! And when we tell you of our journey, you will find it most difficult to believe. These are my other new friends, Eve and Hope. Eve also lived here once, but it was a long time ago."

Noticing the approach of others, Padah turned her head and spotted the jubilant faces of Joy and Grace. Nakeh, also with them, leaned forward, sniffing and nuzzling her affectionately.

"And this," Padah proudly announced, "is Nakeh, my youngest. He is his big brother's most humble keeper!"

Joy, Grace, and Melody declared in unwavering unison, "Yes!"

"Welcome home, Padah. It seemed as if you might never return. We were so thankful when we got word that the kind shepherd had finally found you!" Grace said.

While the sheep continued to share and rejoice in their reunion, the kind shepherd left their side to check on the rest of his flock. Peace, joy, and harmony reigned once again and Padah, thrilled at the sight of Zak and Nakeh, marveled at how much they had grown.

"I suppose there have been a number of changes in my absence," Padah remarked.

"A few. The shepherd has built a new barn next to the house. In fact, it is even larger than the one before and nearly complete now," Joy told her.

"Inviting as that sounds, right now I would give just about anything to revisit the still waters," Padah sighed. "The memory of going there with the kind shepherd gave me hope during the darkest hours of my journey."

"I know that he will take us there very soon, Padah," Joy said.

With a long sigh of both pleasure and tiredness, Padah welcomed the approaching nightfall. Although gloriously happy to be home, she could hardly take in much more. Rest in the presence of the shepherd on the highlands of Menuca was a delicious thought she intended to savor. And now, as the fading sunset drew its rich golden canopy over the western skies, the sweet grasses of the meadow, the cheerful evening chatter of birds overhead, and the soft sounds of the rippling stream off in the distance deeply soothed her soul. This reward was more than she had ever hoped for, and she never intended to leave it again.

"When the Lord brought back
the captives to Zion,
we were like men who dreamed.
Our mouths were filled with laughter,
our tongues with songs of joy.
Then it was said among the nations,
"The Lord has done great things for them."
The Lord has done great things for us,
and we are filled with joy.
Restore our fortunes, O Lord,
like streams in the Negev.
Those who sow in tears
will reap with songs of joy.
He who goes out weeping,
carrying seed to sow,
will return with songs of joy,
carrying sheaves with him."
–Psalm 126 NIV

BEYOND THE GATE

Padah was so tired from the night before, that she did not even notice both Zak and Nakeh had lain down to sleep between Grace and herself. Only upon waking in the morning did she realize their simple act of loyalty.

How sweet, she thought with a bit of sadness. I have lost so much time with them. Before too long my lambs will be grown.

Hearing voices, Padah's attention was drawn to a skirmish in the corner of the barn.

"It's only Zula and Ursula," explained Melody. "They have been squabbling like that ever since a new ram arrived."

"But I thought they were friends."

"I'm not sure they know how to be friends with anyone. Their alliance was formed to intimidate the rest of the sheep. It served them both well until recently. Now they cannot stand one another!"

"Jealousy is such an ugly thing," Padah said. "Let's go out into the open air where the shepherd is. Maybe he will lead us to the meadows."

Casting a glance at the twins who still slept soundly, Padah decided to follow Melody into the warm sunshine.

"Oh, Melody, I am so happy and grateful to be back home. I'm sure I could go for a week without eating and still be content!"

"Shall we put it to the test?" she teased.

The kind shepherd rounded the corner in time to hear the two giggling. He stretched out his hand to give them the usual stroke on the top of their heads and scratch behind their ears. Then, continuing on, he called out, "You haven't forgotten the way to the meeting place have you, Padah? I know how you love the still waters!"

"He always knows my desires, before I even speak them!" she said.

"It's true," Melody agreed.

The two contented sheep waded through the tender, succulent grasses on their way to the meadow. One by one, the rest of the flock joined them. The cloudless sky, the gentle breeze, and the lush green fields all combined to create a perfect day!

By midmorning the gentle shepherd joined the rest of his eager flock. With rod and staff in one hand and a flute in the other, he led them merrily over the meadow's ridge and down the hills that sloped easily toward the stream. As the sound of the nearby rushing waters intensified, so too did the memories of Padah's previous tranquil visit with the shepherd. The refreshing water that cascaded from the Mountains of El Shaddai were intoxicatingly cool and pure. Leaving the world behind them, the satisfied sheep absorbed the soothing sounds of the waves spilling over the rocks while the birds sang and chirped gaily from their perches. Nothing else seemed to exist or even matter.

The flock soon settled down under the familiar trees that faced the stream. The shepherd, however, continued farther down the hill until reaching the large shade trees closest to the edge. Arriving at the designated meeting place, he turned around and called his sheep.

"Eve, Hope, you must come with us to join the shepherd at the meeting place! Naomi, won't you come also?" Padah inquired.

"I am too tired to go that far right now," Naomi said. "I'll join you another time."

"Don't worry, I'll stay back and keep her company," Eve offered.

"No! You don't understand. You will miss a wonderful experience if you don't come. The shepherd will take us to the still waters where only he knows the way," Padah argued.

"There is always next time. Right now we are tired from our walk, so please go on ahead," Naomi said, lowering her head to graze.

Seeing Padah's disappointment, Hope rose to her feet. "I'll come with you and the others."

"You won't regret it!" Padah exclaimed.

Gradually making their way to where the shepherd stood, Hope, Melody, Grace, and Padah ambled single-file down the hill to the edge of the stream. Upon reaching the shepherd's side, Padah noticed that others had joined them as well.

Following the lead of their shepherd, the small group walked along the winding path at the edge of the stream. When they reached the pure headwaters, the shepherd located his favorite large flat rock and sat down. The sheep lay down in the soft grass at his feet, and Padah found her place on his side. She drank in the tranquility and beauty that surrounded her, and a wonderful stillness settled upon her spirit and soul. She allowed herself to be consumed by the overwhelming presence of her shepherd. Pushing aside every other thought, she completely abandoned herself to his love.

Conscious only of the kind shepherd's soft flute playing in the background, Padah rested serenely. Then she heard his voice.

"Padah, you have never been separated from my love. From the day I found you along the roadside, I knew you would be one after my own heart. Your weaknesses I have not counted against you, because I understood the true intent of your heart was to follow after me. I knew your pain and the deep loneliness that often plagued your soul. I have always had plans for you, Padah, but you were not always ready for my plans. You must continue to trust me, no matter what happens. I will never leave you alone, even though it might appear so for a time.

But I have seen your tenacious desire to seek after me, and you have greatly pleased me. Because of this, I intend to restore bountifully all that you have considered lost."

The afternoon spent at the still waters seemed to end much too quickly when the shepherd stood up in preparation for their return.

"It is time," he said. "We have stayed as long as we are able this afternoon. The other sheep are waiting and we must return home before dark."

Patiently he led his contented sheep back up the path toward the gentle slopes where the rest of the flock lingered. Together, they began the long walk back home. At the crest, the shepherd led them south toward the barn. But as the flock drew near, they were unprepared for the danger that awaited them. Entering the shepherd's property, they were met by a large group of men, torches in hand, standing brazenly before them.

"We have been requested by the town's high counsel to return you to the valley for trial. The charges are thievery and fraud. You purposely sought to mislead the inhabitants of the Valley of Achor, withholding from them the only real source of water, jeopardizing every member of the community! We have all paid a terrible price for your greed. You are under arrest, and if you are found guilty, you will be sentenced to death."

Mocking shouts of victory rang out from among the group as they shoved the kind shepherd face-down onto the ground. The angry men tortured him, kicking him from behind, thrusting their torches into his face. Grabbing and yanking his head backward, his hair in their hands, they pulled him up.

"Stand up, you liar!" they shouted. "Walk like the hero you pretend to be!"

Picking up a stone, one of the men hurled it at the kind shepherd's back. A second spat in his face, while still another picked up a stick with which to strike the side of his head. The kind shepherd's face soon dripped blood, his eyes filled with sadness and pain.

Horrified and in a state of disbelief, Padah and the rest of the kind shepherd's flock could hardly bear to watch. Fear filled their hearts. They did not know, nor could they comprehend, that this too was part of the gentle shepherd's plan. They did not see the multitude of white robed figures standing upon the hill behind them.

"Why are they doing this to the kind shepherd?" Nakeh asked. "They don't know him, do they?"

"No, they don't know him at all," Padah whispered.

Padah saw that it was the old man who led the group, and anger flared within her. When, suddenly, Zak lunged through the air, catching the backside of the unsuspecting old man, shoving him with his forehead. Zak disengaged himself just in time for the old man to be slammed face-down in the mud in front of the water tubs.

"That's the way, Zak! You show him!" Nakeh cheered. "Give him another one! Give him one for me!"

Lost in his exuberance, Nakeh leaped triumphantly through the air with his feet kicking up behind him. Then, catching Padah's warning glance, he retreated timidly behind Grace's back leg.

"You will only make matters worse, Nakeh. We must be quiet for now. Zak has acted up enough to put us all on the dinner menu!" Padah whispered.

The townsmen, however, ignored the incident. Instead they took out their unwarranted rage against the shepherd. Shoving him from behind while forcing him down the path, the men took great delight in their abusive behavior. The helpless sheep could do nothing more than look on in sorrow and confusion, while their shepherd disappeared into the distance accompanied by his ruthless accusers.

"He did not even open his mouth to defend himself," Padah thought. He was like a lamb being led to slaughter. Watching her shepherd, she felt a deep emptiness even beyond what she had experienced before, a sorrow too painful for words.

Nearly two hours passed before the kind shepherd's flock, still standing motionless, decided their master would not be returning. Turning their gaze backwards, the muddled sheep began to head for the barn.

Padah remained standing alone. Eventually dropping to her knees she began to weep.

"I do not understand any of this. Without the kind shepherd it is impossible to go on."

She cried until she had no more tears, until eventually she fell into a deep sleep.

In her dream, she saw the early morning sun shine its glory over the soft pink hills of the highlands. And though the morning sun was full of promise, Padah's heart remained empty and without hope—her face wet from tears, and her heart, aching from emptiness within her.

"Shepherd!" she cried. "Where are you? Where have they taken you? I have journeyed so far to find you again…and now this? Why did you let them take you away? Without you, I cannot go on, for you are my reason for living."

Filled with grief, she began to cry once again. But just as the breeze once carried the threat of storm, it now carried whispers of hope refusing to allow her to give up.

"Padah…"

Looking up she saw nothing.

"Padah…"

As she looked up a second time, her eyes noticed a gate left slightly ajar near the entrance of the property.

Strange, she thought to herself. I have never noticed it before. Intrigued by the gate's sudden appearance, Padah got up and walked toward it. She saw that it was beautiful, made of pure gold and decorated with ornate carvings. Peering through the opening she saw two men in white garments beckoning her to come closer.

"Excuse me," she said," but have you seen my shepherd? He is the kind highland shepherd and he was taken away. I fear I might never see him again."

"Oh," the one man answered. "You mean the Great Shepherd, the Shepherd King, the Great Redeemer, the Great I AM , the Lamb of God?"

"Well, I guess that's who I mean," Padah answered, perplexed. "Have you seen him?"

Without saying another word both men pointed down a long golden corridor that looked as if it had no end.

"Shepherd? Shepherd, are you there?" she inquired, waiting for some sort of sign.

Hearing nothing but the faint sound of music in the distance, the small solitary sheep pressed on in her search for answers.

"Padah..."

"It is his voice! I know it is his voice! But wherever could he be? And why is he hiding himself from me?" she asked herself.

A lovely but unearthly fragrance filled her nostrils.

"It is his scent. I know it from when he drew close to me. He is here after all! I just know it is him!" she cried out jubilantly. "Shepherd! Shepherd! Please show me your face. Please let me know where you are!"

Padah's search took her to the end of the corridor through an archway leading into a magnificent, lush courtyard bearing flowering shrubs that Padah had never seen before. Two beautiful golden doors graced the far end of the courtyard. Finding herself drawn to them, she walked forward. As Padah approached, they opened slowly before her. The doors were edged with exquisite and brilliant jewels of every color imaginable. Once through them, she looked down. Under her feet spread a transparent sea of glass that sparkled with light as intense as the sun itself.

Allowing her eyes to travel the full length of the glass, Padah suddenly gasped with surprise. Standing in the center of an unspeakably glorious throne stood a lamb looking as if it had been slain. He was encircled by four living creatures and twenty-four elders, all of whom fell down before the Lamb, each one holding a harp and golden bowl of incense and singing songs of adoration.

"Worthy is the Lamb who was slain to receive power and wealth and wisdom and strength and honor and glory and praise. To him who sits on the throne and to the Lamb, be praise and honor and glory and power forever and ever!"

In awe, Padah herself was unable to stand, but lay face down before the Great Lamb, when she heard a voice saying, "Never again will they hunger, never again will they thirst. The sun will not beat upon them nor any scorching heat. For the Lamb who is in the midst of the throne will shepherd them and lead them to living fountains of water. And God will wipe away every tear from their eyes."

"Padah," the Lamb's voice called to her once again. "Do not fear to come to me."

Unable to move, Padah's sense of unworthiness gripped her as an icy hand that refused to release her from its hold.

"Come to me, Padah," the Great Lamb said, "because I have overcome, so shall you. Be strong and of great courage, for I live forevermore."

The two men dressed in long white robes lifted her gently to her feet. With knees weak and her heart beating wildly, Padah began to walk toward the Great Lamb, whom she now recognized as her shepherd. Smiling, he opened his outstretched arms to welcome her. Padah yearned to bury herself in them. Reaching down to pick her up, her Shepherd King, the Great Lamb upon the throne, embraced her with an intensity of love that filled her heart to overflowing.

Holding her close to his heart he whispered, "You have an inheritance beyond measure reserved for you. Soon my little one, you will sit at my right hand, for you bear my mark. Because you belong to me, all that I have shall be yours as well. You must never again doubt my love or provision for you. When you cry out to me in time of need,

I will always be with you. Though you do not see me with your eyes, I will be by your side. When your heart aches, I will feel it too. When your faith wanes, I will be there to encourage you. And though I know you would like nothing more than to stay with me now, there is much I have yet for you to do. It is needful Padah, that you return to the flock and give them hope of my return. Encourage the others to remain faithful, to not despair."

Wiping away her tears, the Great Shepherd continued to hold Padah for a long time before gently releasing her.

When she reopened her eyes from the deep sleep, she found herself still lying on the ground. Joy, Naomi, and Melody stood peering down at her, their inquisitive gaze demanding an answer, until Naomi finally spoke.

"You have spent an entire night out here, Padah. Your despair has worried us greatly."

"Yes! And the flock has been in a state of shock, wondering what will become of us all. Whatever shall we do now that our kind shepherd is gone?" Melody asked.

Gazing off into the distance as if witnessing something the others could not see, Padah responded, a new confidence evident in her voice.

"We shall wait for his return, for I saw him in a dream as a victorious Lamb. He was mighty in power, reigning upon a great white throne and robed in majesty. He is not dead at all nor has he deserted us, but he lives. We have nothing to fear. All we need to do is call out his name and he will be there.

"It's a strange thing, but I finally realized that even during my long, lonely journey, somehow...the kind shepherd had been with me all the time."

"*Therefore, we who have fled to him for refuge*
can take new courage,
for we can hold onto his promise with confidence.
This confidence is like a strong and trustworthy anchor
for our souls. It leads us through the curtain of heaven
into God's inner sanctuary.
Jesus has already gone in there for us."
–Hebrews 6:18-20 NLT

Thank you for taking the time to read my book, *For the Love of Padah*. Though I will most likely never have an opportunity to meet you personally, it is my deep desire that through this book, you will meet the one who really matters...the ageless Great Shepherd himself.

"But the Lord still waits for you
to come to him so he can
show you his love and compassion.
For the Lord is a faithful God.
Blessed are those who wait for him
to help them."
–Isaiah 30:18 NLT